THE MAN WITH A MIRROR FACE

Mahon McCann

Shinobi Publishing

Copyright © 2020 by Mahon McCann
www.mahonmccann.com

For more information, contact: writing@mahonmccann.com

First paperback edition December 2020

Book Cover by James Carter
Instagram: jamescarterart
www.jamescarterartist.com

Editing by Annie Jenkinson

Author photo by Graham Crichton

ISBN 978-1-8381468-0-1 (Paperback)
ISBN 978-1-8381468-1-8 (eBook)

THE MAN WITH A MIRROR FACE

"Choose the sword, and you will join me... Choose the ball, and you will join your mother in death. You do not understand my words, but you must choose... Son, convoy, choose—life, or death?"

Lone Wolf (Shogun Assassin)

Contents

Acknowledgements..ix

Fifty Shades of Beige..1

So Long, Old Friend...23

Butterfly Man...27

The Whiskey Republic..41

Uncle Bob's Van...61

Milltown Cemetery...83

Love & Moustaches..97

A Great Big Chimp...103

How Not to Get Away with Murder...111

The Forgotten One..121

Launderette for Losers..139

The Man with a Mirror Face...149

About the Author..165

Acknowledgements

I DEDICATE THIS BOOK to the many who have helped and encouraged me along this journey:

To my mom for always reading everything, even though she's the busiest, and my dad, who taught me to believe in miracles and to never sell myself short.

To Siofra, who is always so good for a chat and advice, and Aine, who is more talented than me, and who had better start using it.

To Brendan and Maria, who gave me the money to finish my Masters' and whose love is unconditional and a constant source of strength and reassurance in my life.

To my girlfriend Anna, who has been so patient with my mania and constant demands to read things; you are the best, and I love you.

To Michael and Col and Conan, the brain trust and fellow artists on the journey, pioneers of belief, good advice, and crafty plans; you never steer me wrong.

To my coach Josh and the Muay Thai family, for supporting my writing as well as my martial arts ambitions.

To my friends James, who designed the book's cover, Brian, Chris, Philip, Tony, Conor, Rocher, Tim, Ando, Douglas, Jamie and all the boyos, who will always be the lads.

And to all the fans I have discovered along the way. The people who read and enjoy my work are the only reason it exists and will continue to exist.

My hope is to be able to return the favor of your belief and investment in me by making great art, and as with all endings, this is really only the beginning of something.

Thank you.

Fifty Shades of Beige

EVERYTHING IN OUR HOUSE was beige, clean. Not quite white, but beige.

The walls were beige, the ceilings, the food, the shampoo bottles… even the dog was beige. It all blended in, one beige thing against the next.

So, I grew up in a beige world.

Yet I'd say I was more of a deep crimson—if I had to choose a colour. As a young girl, I wouldn't have minded beige-blonde hair myself, but we were all dark like Mum.

Dad had died when I was young, and Mum—whom we called 'Mam', too, depending on how we felt at the time—had never moved on. She fed all of her anxiety into gardening, chores, and walking the beige dog, weeding and seeding, and doing everything in the world possible to avoid confronting the fact that now, she was alone.

I believed that she still missed Dad, even despite it being so long.

Sometimes, she would stare at his photo, then slowly replace it in its photo frame, on the top of the television. But time had passed as time tends to do, and she was nearly fifty now, and still hadn't found another husband.

Times were getting desperate, and she was at risk of being lonely in old age.

My two older brothers had long since moved out, living in Berlin and Australia, and I was the lucky one who'd just returned home from college to find this hellish mess.

Well, what choice did I have?

The solution was, staring me in the face in fact.

I had to get my mum on Tinder.

"Mam," I said one day over breakfast. I said it while she was distracted washing the dishes, rubber gloves up to her elbows, soap flying everywhere.

"Since you got the new upgrade on your phone, have you tried any new apps at all?"

A moment's silence.

She glanced over her shoulder suspiciously,

"Apps? Do I look like I've time for apps? There's mould on the ceiling! The dog hasn't been walked, and it's about to start raining! Would you take in that washing, love?"

"Look, I was just thinking that maybe now, you might want to try some dating apps... you know? Maybe..." She stopped her dishwashing as though I'd just fired off a gun in the kitchen.

I kind of expected a random plate to go slipping from her grasp onto the tiled floor, and smash. It didn't, but what went into tiny pieces instead was the whole demeanour of her face.

Her eyebrows were all over the place, her nose wrinkled, her eyes wildly scanning the space in different directions, as though they were not a perfectly matching pair.

She was a big woman and had wheeled around to face me now, her expression a cross between disbelief and scorn. She wore the look of a person who was about to let you 'have it' as they say, whatever it was they might let you have.

"What like that, *Tinder?*" she said, throwing back her head and laughing mercilessly. "What age do you think I am? Running around with strange men at night, doing all sorts? That's for all you lunatic young people with your libidos and chat-up lines..."

"First of all... gross, Mam, and you just need to try new things. I'm scared you are getting... Demented." She removed from the soapy stew of the sink a Tupperware box stained slightly orange by spaghetti Bolognese, and began furiously rubbing away at that immortal stain.

She scrubbed at the thing like a woman possessed.

"I am not... I am not demented!" She heaved one mighty leg up on the counter and continued scrubbing as if she was about to start a lawnmower.

"Honestly, I think we're going to have to have you sectioned if you turn any worse."

"Go on, have me sectioned, then! I won't care! They have lovely gardens in the Dundrum Mental Institution, and at least I won't have to put up with you in there, will I? Might get some peace for a change!"

She furiously scrubbed at the Tupperware box with all kinds of scrubbers, pinning the wretched thing down with one hand and pummelling it furiously with the other, as if it had committed some heinous crime against her. I was sure she would continue until the plastic was see-through again, a feat which would have been impossible for anyone else. Others would have given up without even trying, so stubborn was that stain. But Mum never gave up.

"But I'm the best..." I said, with a wry smile.

"The best at annoying me. Now, I've to walk that dog! He's been at me all day! Look at him, moaning and whining to go out..."

The dog's belly rose up and down in the corner as he snored, his four legs worn down to stubs like an old 2H pencil. Poor Rocky had had the legs walked right off him. She'd hauled him up mountains, across lakes, valleys, gorges, through ditches and even across the local tip.

He was going to have a heart attack if things continued this way.

"Look, you're going to kill that dog and me too…" I said, eyeing her phone on the kitchen table. "We can't go on like this…"

It was clear that drastic times called for drastic measures.

"After all the things I've done for you!" Mum said, "the sacrifices! The school runs! The breastfeeding… Oh! Don't get me started on the breastfeeding! I've still got bruises, and nipples down to my ankles thanks to you, and they won't be getting reduced anytime soon…"

"Mam, what is this rant even about? What do you want? I can't even tell anymore!"

Outside the window, vast clouds were gathering and starting to look stormy and threatening. The first few drops of rain were beginning to fall on the tropical rainforest of the back garden.

"The washing line!" she said now, running, grabbing the dog's lead and tugging on her rain jacket. The purple anorak was over her too. Quickly, without thinking, I stood up, snatched her phone and thrust it deep into my pocket. Now, I had possession of it.

"I do the washing… the cleaning… scrubbing the floor… There's nothing in the house which anyone else ever even…" Her head popped out from the hole of the jacket, to see I was already holding the pegs.

She squinted at me suspiciously,

"So, you'll do it then?"

"Of course, Mam, us girls have to stick together, right?"

I gave her a large and dramatic hug.

"Enjoy your walk!"

△▽△

God, I was the devil herself sometimes. I mean, stealing was a crime. But this was for a good cause, and anyway, I was only borrowing the device, and would give it back soon.

You need a few eggs to break an omelette, as they say. But even if I just signed her up, then surely the hard part was done? She'd see the positives and delve deeper into it, find a man, fall in love, get off my back all the time and we'd all live happily ever after, surely?

Musing on it all, I wandered around the house, depositing the washing on the radiators, distributing it nicely and stretching it all out.

Why were radiators always in the most random and inaccessible places?

Behind the couch, under a desk, there they were... And then, you couldn't reach to dust behind them either, so draping the laundry over one always carried a risk it might come back up laden with a nest of dead and crispy spiders.

How was anyone supposed to do anything creative in this boring environment?

Instead, I sat in the office chair and twirled around maniacally. All throughout my uni life, I had been perched on Tinder like a hungry spider, with one guy who would take me out for dinner, another for drinks, free cinema, bowling... one even did my weekly shopping for me.

Let's just say I went on a bit of a *rampage*, as Mum put it.

She, on the other hand, would be more careful, conservative, really.

Her own generation was reputed to be full of wild ones compared to their own mothers', but women the age of my mam generally thought half a bottle of peach schnapps and a drag off a joint was going mental. Well, in that case, I was only glad she couldn't see what I'd gotten up to on my *rampage*. The way she had been brought up also meant that the concept of online dating was still out there. Hence, no chance of relying on Mum for any help whatsoever!

So, I would soon find that while setting up a Tinder profile for myself was daunting enough, drafting one for Mum would be even tougher. OK, so, where to begin?

Likes and dislikes... section one. It seemed as good a place to begin as any other.

Well, Mum had hobbies, and lots of them. Didn't she? Hobbies such as... umm... Now my brain was already working overtime. Did she honestly have any interests at all?

Walking the dog? Cleaning? Tweaking the muck out of the kitchen tiles with a toothpick? Scrubbing Tupperware?

How did anyone hope to make any of this sexy and alluring? This was all too hard, and I was beginning to wish I'd never 'volunteered' to do it. She didn't even want the goddamned thing, and here I was, maxing out my creativity and giving myself a gutload of stress.

And then there was the issue of photographs! Should I use old ones, in which she looked sublimely slim and beguiling, with sultry eyeliner and funky clothes?

Or new ones, in which she looked like—well, looked like anyone's mom, really, only with wild eyebrows that should have been trimmed back eons ago, before they'd come to monopolize her face like hungry caterpillars.

If you took the pictures from the 1970s, you'd technically be a catfish.

The temptation to go wild and be a Joseph Goebbels, making Mum out to be some sort of lunatic was strong, but I restrained myself. I used her phone to take photos of the mantelpiece's pictures, and then dug out some old ones. Last, I unearthed one or two recent ones for context.

It was funny going through the pictures, seeing her and Dad together, happy, my brothers as babies, and a whole family, reunited. In some ways, looking at these reminded me how Dad had really been, what kind of a man he was, and give a hint as to what she might look for in a new man. Dad had been a bit of a square with glasses and brownish-blond hair.

I was sure she would want a nerdy type of a man, someone after companionship as well as a steady, stable relationship kind of a thing—a partner to walk the dog together, or something like that. That was it! Eureka, I had it! In her bio section of the profile, always the trickiest bit—where you didn't want to look boring but also not up your own hole—I was going to put, *I love walking the dog, so I do.* A stupid grin traversed my face. This must have been how Michelango felt when he painted the Mona Lisa, flawless.

I could hardly contain myself when Mum arrived back in the house, leaping up from the couch and hurtling back into the kitchen to show her what I'd done for her. Photos, a bio, everything... there they all were, ready to go!

"Look it's this easy, Mam... I've done all of it for you!"

She nearly dropped the lead onto Rocky's head. If she had, he probably would have been thankful for the excuse to return to his dreams.

"What the hell is that!"

Proudly, I swiped through the images.

"Mam, that's you before you became an old and boring fart! Anyway, it's not so long ago," I said, smiling.

"Ah stop. Wouldja just look at that!"

She set the clothes down on the table, leaning in close, squinting and the screen and momentarily transfixed by the old photos she probably hadn't seen in years.

She smiled, and some of the wrinkles and lines of worry receded.

If only she would just say yes and give it a go, the possibilities were endless. I envisioned having the house to myself at the weekend, and parties would be possible, and then there'd be all the allowance money from her new boyfriend. Living the dream, really.

"Look, this is your profile, Mam... and then to see who you can pick, just click here. Yep, now if you swipe right on them, that..."

She swiped right on 'John, 32', like a biblical verse, showing a photo of him with some sports car in Marabaya. That car probably wasn't even his, a real lemon if I'd ever seen one. "You just *liked* him, Mam..." I said, giving her a playful nudge with my elbow.

"Oh God, you're kidding! I didn't mean to do that! *Like* him? I don't even know him! And I mean, he's, like... Like, it's a nice picture, so it is, but *thirty two?* I'm not a cradle snatcher..."

She started panicking. "So what now, Shan? Does he get my address? He's going to come round here? Do I have to go out with him? I mean, has that even sent a message to him? Am I going to have to say no to him? What if he wants... I'm too old for... Oh, never mind. But Shan, stop! Take it away! Turn it off! I don't want any part in this! It's way too dangerous... What if he just turns up?"

A mad fit of laughter bit at my belly, and I couldn't stop laughing. Did she really believe all that stuff?

"No, Mam. He only swipes back, and even then if he messages you, you don't have to do anything." She collapsed into a chair in the kitchen with the force of relief. The legs of the chair scraped on the hard floor.

"I don't get it, Shannon. This is awfully complicated. It's not how things were in my day." She said it as if she was ninety-five, not fifty-ish.

And she was stressed now, but what else was new?

"You have to join the 21st century someday," I said.

The dog farted on the kitchen floor. "See even Rocky agrees..." I added.

She snatched back her phone.

"No means no!" I sagged down, deflated.

"Please, Ma, just give it a go?"

"Oh, go on then. Maybe. Now get out of here before I change my mind!"

I couldn't spend all my time worrying if Mum was going to continue with her digital dating or not, as I had my own bad romance to worry about. There was this guy, Charlie, who I'd been seeing. He seemed interesting, creative, attentive... and so, I'd been thinking about ghosting him. Sometimes, I just took a notion and cut one of them off. There were so many, and it was impossible to fit them all in. I'd have to keep a schedule and fix up appointments soon to avoid them all showing up at the same time.

Who could keep count of this sort of thing, anyway? And everyone was so boring on these sites, so just one was more than adequate— and at times, I couldn't even be bothered with one either. Last time I'd checked, there were 1000 matches. It all made me wonder, what was the point in ever settling down if a girl could have one man a week for the rest of her life?

△▽△

Rules for a first date on Tinder were simple. Somewhere bright, well lit, with lots of people in case he turned out to be a serial killer; you never could tell with boys, or at least I couldn't, and I thought Mum would be just as clueless. So, you also needed an exit strategy, a girl who could whisk you away with a phone call in case things got weird.

One minute, he'd seem fine, and then the next, he was trying to finger you in the parking lot, and then you'd to delete his number off your phone.

So, when did I decide to have sex with a boy?

Well, sometimes, I didn't at all.

Sometimes, there was just no way I was having sex with anyone ever again, because it was all so tedious and unappealing, and messy, a whole lot more bother than it was worth. Other times, there could literally be a piece of drywall and the dance floor, and I'd go, *yep*.

I was selective, though, *really* selective...

And I *could* say no; it was just that I hadn't been saying it, that's all.

And anyway, for a long time, I'd actually been in a relationship with this guy, my first proper boyfriend, a super-cool gym guy, and we were in love. Well, I was…

But I'd never felt as though I could get properly close to him, like, intimate and loved-up, not quite like other girls with their boyfriends. Truth was, if you saw us in public, you'd probably think we were just friends, or—even worse—brother and sister.

And then I found out he'd been cheating on me for ages, so yeah… It all made sense now, and I was broken inside and couldn't ever have a happy relationship again.

Boys sucked, and I really wished I could be like Mum and not care about them, just walk the dog and do the dishes, and not give a feck.

Maybe I'd take a break from boys altogether, then, and have a bit of me time?

The door burst open and Mum was there, still in her dressing gown, eyes wide and she looked so bedraggled. "Aagh! I've got a match! I've got a match! What do I do?" she shouted.

I screamed with laughter. So much for not being interested, then.

She was the same way she always was with technology: flustered.

I squinted at the small screen, eyeing his photograph. Her match was nothing special; a slightly younger guy, mid-forties, named Donal. He was a chartered accountant who enjoyed fishing, philanthropy, and a glass of brandy on the holidays. A real firecracker, then. And in every one of his photos, he wore the same shirt, bootcut jeans, the occasional suit. But at least he had hair, unlike most others. Donal had, however, messaged her an instant classic.

"Are you well?" he said, "cause you're looking well!"

"Eww, gross," I told Mum. "Mam, don't reply to that."

"Why not?" Mum said, "It's rude not to reply."

"Yeah, but that line is basic and if you don't like somebody on Tinder, you just ghost them. Don't say anything."

"Yes, but I'm not a ghost! I don't *ghost* people and I'm not about to start now. Shan, where are your manners? Are you doing this to people?"

I fell silent. The last thing I wanted was a lecture about being rude to people on the internet, especially not when it was people I didn't know and didn't much care about.

"Yes that's in real life, Mam. But Tinder isn't real life. He has to put in some effort, say something clever or witty..."

"I think that's very witty..."

"Because you have hopeless taste..."

"You wouldn't think you were so picky with the amount of fellas walking through that door! I was under the impression if they had a pulse, you'd let them in."

The cheek!

"Mother, I do have options, ok?" I took out my phone, waving it before her eyes. "Look at all these matches." I scrolled through the hundreds and hundreds of potential suitors, and Mum shook her head.

"But you only need one."

"Well, of course, but you want the best one, surely!"

"Then why do you keep picking the ones with clothes that don't fit? The ones with the arses of their pants somewhere around their knees..."

"Oh Mam! That's the style."

"Style indeed... Some *style* that is, then."

She showed off a picture of Donal in a business suit at his company's annual dinner for Autism. "He's got style," she claimed, her eyes twinkling as if she was already quite smitten.

I gave up. There was no talking to this conservative woman who'd quite obviously been brainwashed by her traditional upbringing, and I would have to pull this Donal chap for her now. I was going to wash my hands of the whole thing.

"So, what are you going to message him back then? 'Fine, how are you?'"

"Yes that's good. Should I sign my name at the end, like a text message? Like, 'Thanks. Fine, how are you? Deirdre'. Just so he knows who it is? Is that how you do it?"

"My God, Mam. You must be one hundred years old."

"Hey, stop being mean. This is all new, ok? At least I can use the washing machine without turning everybody's clothes pink!"

"That was one time I did that with the washing! Once! Four years ago! Why do you even still remember that?"

"Maybe because my work blouse hasn't been the same since..."

"Well, I only hope the menopause doesn't make me mental like you. Try something a little more risky, ok? A little more playful... Right?"

She started typing at one mile an hour and stopped,

"Jesus, Mary and Joseph. I think I need to get my glasses for this..."

△▽△

After a couple of days of what was probably a toenail-curling conversation, the date was set, at Costa Coffee overlooking Nutgrove Shopping Center. It wasn't exactly Paris or Rome, but at least she was getting going. Costa was located in the old Circuit gym, overlooking Loreto crossroads, McDonalds and Nutgrove Park. I had advised her to indulge in some alcohol to loosen up proceedings, but Mum hadn't drunk since morning sickness with me in the year 2000, and I didn't really want to revisit that conversation again. I was sitting on the stairs, playing firewoman while Mum tried getting dressed in her room.

"What look am I going for, Shan?" she complained. "What should I wear?"

"Clothes preferably, Mother." I checked the dirt under my fingernails, and she came barreling out of her room, holding a beige turtleneck.

"Mum, really? Beige? Do you not have anything *colourful?*"

"No, you're rushing me to go and do this, and I've had no preparation. No, nothing, I've half a mind not to go..." She was right. After all, I was the architect of this steaming disaster. Was I beginning to regret meddling in her business? No, I wasn't, as the poor dog was one walk away from cardiac arrest, and the garden was like something off the National Geographic.

My mother needed to loosen up and have some fun.

And I was the one who would have to force her to do it!

"I don't even know what to say," Mum complained. "I haven't been on a date in thirty years. The last person I went on one with was your father! We went to see Blade Runner, and it was terribly violent, and he said, 'But they're only robots...'

"But I still couldn't agree with it and so we got up and left, and then he got hit by a bus..." Now, her voice hitched and big tears were rolling down her cheeks. This film was thirty-odd years ago and she was still going to cry! This was not going particularly well.

"Look, the beige isn't that bad, but what about your white cardigan that's nice?" I came to her side to comfort her. We were hardly ever this close. I had my dad's genetics and she was nearly half a foot taller than I was, so I reached up and patted her head.

"Mum, definitely no crying on this date anyway. Crying is not good etiquette for a first date. Look, this guy probably has all sorts of baggage of his own. He's a divorced middle-aged man from that generation of men that lost everything in the crash. He's divorced, depressed, and you'll probably look like a little ray of sunshine compared to what he's been through."

She laughed and sniffed, wiping tears on her sleeve.

"I can't even remember how to do my makeup... Do you think I should do my makeup?"

"Yes!" I said, "that's it!" I rushed into my room and grabbed what I could. A little skin tone and blusher, mascara around the eyes, and she actually looked pretty good.

I was impressed with myself.

Now for the final touch, a hint of sweet and glossy red on the lips.

"Are you sure, Shan? I haven't worn lipstick in ten years! Isn't bright red a little...you know...?"

"Tarty?"

"Well... it isn't, is it? How do I look?"

"Mum you look great, and no, you do not look tarty. Honestly."

I was not one for the compliments, so she knew I was serious.

"Shan, I don't know if I can do this. It just feels so weird, and your father..."

"Dad is gone, Mum," I said in a low voice. "He isn't coming back; *you* need to move on. For your sake, Mum. Dad would want that."

A lump caught in my own throat, knowing this was still hard for her, and she missed Dad.

I felt like a real hard-ass, forcing her out the door like this, still in my dressing gown. Part of me felt downright rotten, but I knew it was for her own good.

"I guess so..."

"Come on, out you go."

"There's stew in the fridge if you get hungry, Shan. You might have to defrost it, but you know how to do that in the microwave? I can come back in and show y—"

"Mum!" I interrupted. "It's one evening, not a lifetime! I'm not going to starve to death. OK, goodbye, Mam…" Then I realised something else I hadn't said.

I opened the door a sliver again, and called, "And have fun!"

Now, I shut the door and rested against the frame for a moment, sighing.

Weirdly, I had a bad feeling about this one…

I lifted the stew from the freezer. The brown mince had turned a lightish grey in the icy abyss, and I threw the dinner in its reused Chinese take-away tray on the hob to defrost.

In the absence of Mum, there were only my own thoughts to turn to, and they weren't great. Painful, even. The dog padded over, his nails clicking against the kitchen's tile floor, and I rubbed his head, ruminating. What was I going to do all evening? How could I forget about Mum's sad face? If only I had pints… But I didn't. What was the next best thing? The dog panted warm breath on my hand, then rubbed his wet nose into my leg. Then he let out a bark,

"You've already been walked today, haven't you?" He barked again. "Hasn't she already dragged you around town…"

He barked, jumping, seemingly excited as he looked at his lead.

"Jaysus, Mum might be right about you. You really are demanding…"

△▽△

Jaysus! Now here was I, walking the dog to relieve my anxiety. It was as if Mum had left, and suddenly, I had turned into her. Now I was Mum! I shuddered at the thought!

We trundled around the field in Ballinteer, the dog and I, following along the river which might have been the Dodder. I knew this was where my ex lived, and truth be told, I purposely avoided this place because of all that. My ex and I had been kind of going out together all through school, sort of secondary-school sweethearts sort of thing.

And then going to college, we'd known we couldn't go on, and maybe that was why he did what he did? Was it my fault?

Some things were better left unsaid, better being avoided at all costs, buried and never to be revisited. But I had reopened my mind to the memories now, and they were flooding back. Suddenly, the thought of even messaging Charlie came back again, another distraction, something to ease the heartache for a minute. Next, I passed by my ex's house, a place that I used to be excited to visit, a place that was so happy. There were memories there, in the front room and kitchen, like ghosts, far away and distant. I could never touch anyone again, and so it suddenly made sense how Mum felt, when Dad wasn't there for her anymore.

It wasn't a case that time healed, I knew that for sure. That was just something stupid, glib, and meaningless that folk would say to try and make you feel better. But it was a filthy lie.

There was always something cruel about having to love more than one person, as if the whole world had to end and start all over again, from scratch—the whole painful process. I could certainly see why Mum must have felt so weird about the whole thing.

Imagine being with someone for twenty years and then starting all over again?

It was hard enough after one. My mind was somewhere else now, wandering, lost…

The dog veered too close to the bushes outside my ex's house, and I found myself tugging at his lead in the right direction, down the hill, towards Nutgrove Shopping Center.

Instead, he pulled me into the front garden, smelling something familiar.

I tried to tug the lead, but it was already too late.

"Rocky! Rocky! Come back!" I was already in his garden, and through the window, there on I could see the couch where we used to always sit on together, my-ex and I.

I tugged Rocky's lead as hard as I could, till he let out a yelp and ran off in the opposite direction.

"I need to get over this..." I whispered under my breath.

I could see the circular dome of Costa Coffee at the bottom of the hill below.

In a lot of ways, I now wished I'd never met my-ex.

On our first date, I'd felt awkward, out of place, but had no way out. But by then, it was already too late.

If only someone had been there to bail me out, the way I had been there for Mum.

△▽△

I checked my watch and grabbed my phone; I was supposed to be there for Mum!

I texted back Charlie and got him to pick me up.

He drove an Opel Corsa which was completely shit, but I didn't even have my license, so kept my mouth shut. He was a nice guy again, all, *where do you want to go? Hey how are you?* Boring! But still, he was here for me and I needed him to give me a lift. I only hoped I was not too late. We pulled into the car park and sat beneath the edge of Costa Coffee, probably 100 meters away, across the road. At such an angle, you would be able to see in without being seen.

"So, why are we here?" Charlie asked, which was a fair enough question.

You receive a message from a random girl who has been ignoring you for ages, and suddenly, you are expected to come running? He had done, so now I was suspicious of him...

"Nope," I said. "Just seems a good spot for sitting in."

Meanwhile, I was craning my neck out the window to see up at the pair of them.

"You know," he said, "I'm kind of surprised that you messaged me back? Didn't seem like you were that interested, really. I've had such bad luck with women lately, and I'm just out of a relationship."

The dog sat in the back of the car, chaperoning the two of us.

Charlie had dark hair and apologetic brown eyes. He was still a nice guy, just not my type. What even was my type at this stage? Whoever would cause me the most amount of emotional damage and was the least suitable for a long-term relationship?

Yep, definitely not this guy, who couldn't damage a puppy. How boring.

Mum and Donal were sitting at a table near the window.

"Can we drive about 100 metres to the right?"

He'd given her a massive bouquet of roses, and she was awkwardly holding still them in front of her body, entirely blocking the view. Good Lord, this was painful. Should I text her?

It would be like one of those undercover dating shows, where the dater wore an earpiece in receipt of secret advice from an expert. "You're definitely looking at something," Charlie said. "Can you to tell me what's going on?"

"Alright, Charlie, look. I'll level with you. My ma is on a date with some guy up there, and I have very good reason to suspect that he is, in fact, a *serial killer.*"

Well, not a very good reason. In fact, no reason, but that was still reason enough. I mean, that was way too many roses for a first date. *What was your angle, Donal?*

"What!" he said seriously, the way I never expected he could be. "Then why are we sitting here? Should we not go get her away from him? Or call the police?"

"Well no, we don't have any evidence, and he might have seduced her already!"

"That makes no sense, but OK," Charlie said, and set his brown eyes to the task of searching for evidence of an impending murder. But to all appearances, this looked like a normal date.

They were drinking coffee, and Mother was twirling her hair.

What?

MOTHER WAS TWIRLING HER HAIR!

But Mother *didn't* twirl her hair?

Jaysus!

This Donal was a smooth operator, then, probably some sort of black widower who went through masses of lonely single women, killing them off for their state pensions. Not that this would ever amount to much, just enough to keep them in underpants and socks...

"I think something's happening..." Charlie said.

He was right. Suddenly, Mum had a hand clasped over her mouth. She was heavily crying, and Donal was stretching across the table, trying to comfort her. Even the waitress looked worried. Mum pushed the flowers aside and hit the gas, and now she was headed for the door.

She leaped into her car and sped away.

"Charlie, follow that car..."

"A *please* would be nice..."

I felt kind of bad for him. This certainly was an unusual first date the two of us were having as adults now, pursuing my mother at high speed through Dundrum. I kind of wished we wouldn't follow her to be honest, and I sure didn't think I was ready to see what I saw next.

We followed her for a couple of miles into Dundrum, where she parked up next to the library and got out. "Where's she going?" Charlie said.

I sighed and unlocked the car door for Rocky, who ran out ahead knowingly, down the winding path to the cemetery above. I knew where she was going.

Dad was buried there, in the cemetery in Dundrum, in a little plot near the front. It was an old graveyard, kind of exclusive as cemeteries went, very much in demand.

The only reason he'd got in was because his own parents—and their parents—had been buried there before him. Sure enough, Mum was right there, crying her eyes out at his graveside. She was surprised to see me, and I traipsed over and lurked beside her. Maybe with another mother and daughter, there'd be a tearful hug and a sob, and we would stand there with our arms around each other. But we weren't like that, not at all. Truth be told, we'd always had a kind of rivalry; I thought she was so old-fashioned, conservative and a do-gooder, while I was, well, the rebel of the family.

"Well, how'd it go?" I asked her from a distance hearing her sniffle.

"How do you think?" she snorted.

She side-eyed me as if I was an evil person, a daughter from hell.

"At least you tried," I supposed. "It's scary putting yourself out there."

Rocky returned from smelling the wilderness, which put her in a better mood, and she bent down and scratched his head. "You actually walked the dog?" she said. It was a stupid question, and obvious that I was walking the dog, but I humoured her for a change.

"Yeah, that dog has had plenty of walking, but he's a real handful... Now I see what you put up with."

"I told you...I'm just not ready yet, Shan," Mum said and shook her sad head. "I don't know if I ever will be. But, you know, thanks..."

"For what?" I felt and sounded defensive, and was on guard.

"For trying," she said. "I know you meant well."

"You don't ever know for sure," I said softly, pleased at the unusual warmth between the two of us. "Mam, you just try, and that's that. Sometimes you get it right, and sometimes you get it wrong, but you always learn something. Isn't that right, Da?" I said into the air, hoping Dad would somehow hear me. Now, I was thinking back to the times that I'd wanted to quit too, and remembered that he had said, 'Nope. Keep going kiddo.' I guessed I missed him more than I thought, and could only imagine how Ma felt, having spent her whole life with one person, and where the love had been reciprocated. How did you ever replace that?

At this moment, I thought maybe a relationship did mean something after all.

And maybe I shouldn't treat mine like pennys' pyjamas, getting hundreds just because they were cheap. "Be pretty nice if Dad were still around? Wouldn't it?"

"It would, alright."

Nothing more needed to be said between us. Dad's aura filled the space.

"Oh," I said to Mum, suddenly, and grabbed hold of her sleeve. Stuck on the cuff of the beige turtleneck was a thorn. I whipped the rose thorn loose and flicked it into the overgrown grass and weeds of the graveyard where thorns belonged.

"The beige looks nice though. Honestly, what was he thinking really? Roses? For a first date?"

"Ah, he was sweet, Shan. It wasn't his fault. He's a nice man."

"You old people are so *weird!* If a guy brought me roses on even the sixth date, I'd think he was a freak."

"The older you get, the more you appreciate these things, darling. And have you ever even gotten to a sixth date? They'd have a better chance with Simon Cowell really."

"Mum, stop."

"Hey. I'm just teasing. Who's that other one you've brought with you now, though?"

I looked back at Charlie in the car, waiting patiently.

"An accomplice. Maybe unwittingly."

Ma laughed. "Gowan, I'll take the dog. I could use a walk after all that excitement…"

"Thanks Mum, for everything."

So Long, Old Friend

THE DOG'S EYES WERE white and milky, her black muzzle turned a silver grey with age.

"Today's the day," Margaret said to the hallway of the apartment, empty except for the dog. She always spoke with the dog. She said good morning to her, and goodnight in the evening; they were family. The dog was named Frieda, after the artist Frieda Kahlo.

Frieda rose slowly to her haunches and padded over.

She stood there, rubbing her head against the dangling lead.

"No," Margaret said, "We aren't walking today."

Poor dear, she thought, *if only there were another way?* But she didn't look so bad; it was just that she hadn't walked all week, not even stood much. Her kidneys were failing and the vet said it was only a matter of time. She was in a lot of pain, and it wouldn't be long now.

Frieda was nearly sixteen, a good run for a dog, Margaret reminded herself.

That's all you could ask for.

When Margaret had first got Frieda, the puppy was only as tall as a blade of grass and everyone in school wanted to hold her. "Oh, isn't she cute!"

Frieda was a boxer mix; mixed with what, they didn't know, but she was boxer mostly. She was good natured, everyone said. And of course, Frieda had seen her through her senior years, and here they were now, at the door. Margaret clipped the lead to her best pal's collar and led the old girl to the doorway. Outside was her car, a little blue Ford Fiesta which Frieda hated because she knew the car meant going to the vets. She would get in though despite her fear, especially if you poked and prodded her, because she trusted Margaret.

And yet it was Margaret who was going to have her killed off.

"Don't look at me like that," Margaret said to Frieda.

"You got old; what am I supposed to do about it?" She had been fighting herself for weeks, seeing the dog deteriorate. When was the right time? The vet said she would know it instinctively, that the right time had come.

But so far, she hadn't gotten farther than the local park.

Who could choose this sort of thing?

She didn't want to let Frieda suffer, but each time she tried to get the old dog to the vets, she couldn't. She tempted Frieda into the driver's seat, giving her a treat, and there they were again, on the edge of life and death, past and future, two aligned souls, sharing final hours.

They were on the way again, to do the thing that couldn't always be deferred, to do the deed, but the day was nice.

It was one of those mornings left over from the summer, one which fell into autumnal months, where the robin redbreasts still skated around collecting morsels to sustain them through the winter, and kids walked the length of Merrion Street Upper on their way to St Stephen's Green. It was autumn and the leaves were dying after the hard work of being green all summer long. When she had failed in her past attempts to get to the vets, Margaret had then taken Frieda to the park in St. Stephen's Green. Frieda loved that place when she was younger, and would spend time sniffing the trees, picking fights with squirrels, making spontaneous and fleeting friendships and rivalries with the other dogs. She had lived the life, old Frieda.

Her hips sank low now as she slinked along the street, a monument to a time that no longer existed. You could count each one of her ribs in the sunlight, too, and Margaret felt dreadfully guilty. Death disturbed her, and she couldn't see over its edge, like going off the side of the world. Who knew how it was, really? Ever since she was a kid, she had been kept awake at night by the thought. It was wrong, selfish to keep Frieda going, but sometimes, as she had seen before, the dog recovered. Then, she spontaneously bounded around like a puppy, as if granted a new lease of life. So, maybe? The doctors, though, said there was no chance.

Not this time.

Margaret watched the people on the street, some smiling, some idly chattering, and many not thinking, not paying attention to their mortality. Those people were free.

But she was no longer free. She was in chains as much as Frieda was.

The park itself was quiet so early in the morning.

A gorgeous morning, another of the summer's residual gems.

The trees and grass were glistening, covered in a light dew, which Margaret wiped away to take a seat next to the pond. The water there was skirted by a little black handrail which the ducks clambered over to beat the seagulls to the breadcrumbs. Anyway, she wouldn't walk far, not now. Frieda's breathing was labored and as soon as she sat to catch her breath, so did the old dog; it just wasn't like her. Margaret reached down and rubbed her head.

A big bruiser of a British bulldog bounded over and gave Frieda a sniff, but she barely raised her head to greet him. Years ago, she would have fought, barked, played, anything. It was selfish, Margaret knew that; she had never married and she and Frieda had been like spinsters, sisters even. Well, everybody else was dead by now—her parents, her friends...

Why shouldn't she die too? Then Frieda would also not be alone wherever she was going.

"I'm sure God will look after you," she said to Frieda, though. "He really must..."

She wondered if there was a doggy heaven, a great big park with green grass and pink, soft chewy toys. She could just wait until nature took its course, letting the decision be made for her, in another week, a day, an hour... Why shouldn't they wait and see?

Some of Frieda's hair blew away in the light breeze, and she thought about the dog lying in bed all day, in constant pain, a shadow of herself. But death? Surely, anything was better than death? A robin flitted over from the trees and seized a clutch of Frieda's hair, escaping to the branches and presumably back to its invisible nest between the leaves. *Early for a robin,* she thought, although they had been known to make nests as early as January.

The start of a long winter?

Maybe he knows something we don't, she thought, *the robin, that is.* She sat for a few moments in silence, enjoying the cold of the morning and the warm dog beneath.

"Ok," she said softly, stirring the old dog, "it's time to go..."

Butterfly Man

THIS IS A STORY about a wall. No ordinary wall, either. This was the highest in the known world. You've heard of the Great Wall of China, the Berlin Wall, even Trump's wall, but the wall at the end of Marley Drive never made the histories, until now. To be fair, my experience of walls was limited to this one, being eight years old and everything. I might have been biased, of course. The story fell within that summer of the late nineties when I fell and broke my arm in two pieces. The older boys of the street had taken to climbing the wall and hanging out in the 'dirt track' beyond. They came back with such fantastical stories of fights and bangers and fires and shop sweets, that I didn't know what to think. What was over there? Little boy heaven?

Until I heard those stories, I had been quite content with my cul de sac, but now it was like a t-shirt I had outgrown. What sort of world was over the wall? What was I missing out on?

I didn't know; I wasn't tall enough to climb the damn thing.

I had spent the summer below my comrades' ankles, Stuart and his older brother Podge.

Podge was the first one over the wall, and he had brought all the others with him.

Stuart was sympathetic to me, having only just hit a growth spurt himself, but it always seemed that just as I was getting going, Podge got in the way.

"Try your foot there..." Stuart added from atop the wall as I flailed down below.

"Come on, Stuart. Leave him! He'll never do it!" Podge told his younger brother. My blood was boiling; easy for him to say with his bloody long legs. Podge was nearly sixteen.

After months of being humiliated, I had concocted a plan to attain my success. There was a spiky tree with black bark and tiny green spiny prickles, one the lads called the 'helping tree.' On this tree were three thick and sturdy branches that could support a boy's weight, like a ladder that would lead to the lip of the wall. At the top, you had to let go of the tree and jump free about a foot, towards the yellow brick of the wall. On either side of the bushes were two tall and swaying pampas grasses, with feather duster hairdos and whip-like vines.

I'd had the displeasure of once being cut by one of these vines, which had left a grotesque paper cut, opened like a tiny mouth. I didn't want any more of those, so I stood on the rough, stony ground beneath the tree and took stock. My stomach felt queasy.

I had never been that high in my whole life? Could I do it?

"He's a bottler," Podge said, marshaling the other boys into formation on the wall before they would leave as they always did. "Watch him quit."

This time, I was determined that I wouldn't quit. I put a foot on the first branch and started to climb, but didn't get very far. I grabbed hold of the wrong branch and came tumbling back down to earth, narrowly avoiding the whiplike pampas, but, instead, landing on the hard, stony ground at the foot of the tree. And there, my arm snapped like the branch it had just clutched onto a moment before.

On the bright side, I had never been in the back of an ambulance before, which was exciting.

"Six weeks," the doctor said, rapping on the side of my new hardened caste with his hairy knuckles. "He's lucky really..."

I didn't feel lucky. I felt cursed.

"Don't worry, doctor. He won't be climbing trees anymore," my mum said and pinched my arm. I stood up obediently and we left the doctor's office for the car that was parked outside. My mother applied the child lock as I got in, to add an extra insult to me, or Da. She still didn't trust me. When I was younger, I used to love opening the door of the car while we were driving. It just caused such a fuss; suddenly, everyone would be screaming and shouting, and we had to pull over to the side of the road. It was magic, really. I couldn't help myself as a young boy, and anything that was dangerous or caused trouble, I was into it!

It didn't take long to get home. The sun was beating down on the driveway and Da was parked halfway under his classic muscle car, and all that could be seen of him were his blue jeans poking out, covered in holes and oily stains. He pushed himself out from under the car engine and wiped the grease from his hands on a rag.

He admired my cast. "Nice war wound," he said.

"Good of you to be around to take him. I thought you were working?"

"I am," he said and pointed to the car.

"You'd rather work on that car than collect your son from the hospital?"

"He's tough," Da said and tousled my hair. Mother shook her head and returned inside.

"You alright?" he asked, and I nodded.

Even if I hadn't been fine, I still wouldn't have said so.

"I'm taking the car out for a spin. Wanna come?" Da said, and I held my arm out again as if to say, 'no fun allowed.'"

"Ah, it'll be grand," he said and touched my shoulder. "Don't you worry about that. Just hop in." The interior of the Trans Am was more like an American diner on wheels than a car. It smelt of leather, had no seatbelts, and the radio pounded out quick, disorienting African Jazz like an old school jukebox. People on the street would look and point and call their friends, and I always felt like a bit of a celebrity sliding around in the front seat.

Dad didn't pay much attention to the rules of the road or to me. He just talked.

He talked about the past, lessons, what not to do, what to do, fights, and people he didn't like. I didn't pay much attention but would often say yes or no, just so he thought I was listening and not being rude. "I listened to this in the seventies," he said. "We were a wild bunch back then, your Mum and I. Those were the days! I even had long hair, wore a full jumpsuit..."

I nodded, smiling.

He carried on.

"Can you believe it?"

I could, since he had never been one to run with the crowd, my Da.

He had no t-shirt on right now, and yet it was probably no more than ten degrees.

He reached over and lit a cigarette from the car's chunky lighter. He never stopped talking when we were together; he was like a shark, swimming.

Often, I wondered if he thought I was a mute or just too shy to form sentences of my own. Either way, he absolved us both of the responsibility—me of speaking, and he of listening.

"We'll have to teach you how to climb properly. So you never fall. *I* never fall. Anyway, I've been saying to get rid of those trees for years. That's what I told Mr. Snellack, to paint the wall and get rid of the trees and we'll have no problems ever again. But he doesn't believe me..." Suddenly, he turned and was very interested, looking at me curiously,

"Don't expect anything from anyone in this world, son. You can't trust them," he said, taking a thick drag of his cigarette. I spent a lot of time listening since I spoke very little.

Most of the time, it was like listening to a song playing in the background, but sometimes, I had an almost schizophrenic moment, when the lyrics were more than just the words.

It was as if someone, or something, was speaking through people like a ventriloquist's dummy, giving me just the message I needed to hear right then.

"Sure, look at Mr. Snellack," he said. "That poor crippled bastard at the end of the road wouldn't hurt a fly, but got burgled and robbed! In a wheelchair, housebound, and they crawl over that back wall, and rob his gaff? Human beings," he said, turning the big steering wheel and looking over shoulder. "More like monsters if you ask me."

Well, that was the first I'd heard of it.

I didn't know the Butterfly Man had been robbed. That was what I called him, because one day, my mother had come home from his house and said, "That poor old man, he's all knotted up like a butterfly." I didn't know what she meant as I had never seen a butterfly that was knotted. Like, its wings were tangled up? Plus, I had never seen him either.

She said he lived in his chair, and that his only friend was his TV set, and his carer was a mean man who smelt of cigarettes and never smiled. And they had stolen his TV set too. Now, he had nothing. That must be pretty bad, and I had empathy since I knew how it was to sit around doing nothing all day, being bored. Since I'd broken my arm, I'd done nothing but play video games till I had big dark rings around my eyes and they didn't seem fun anymore.

Da was never around to give out to me, and Ma had all but given up, or so I thought. I convinced myself that friends didn't matter, the wall didn't matter, nothing mattered.

Why would it? Exactly.

△▽△

I was excited when I awoke and it was a Saturday. For the fourteenth day in a row, I was set to play video games and eat junk food. There were some perks to being injured, and a never-ending excuse for slovenliness was one. The problem was, just as the PlayStation screen was loading and that blissful amber diamond appeared, my mother would always knock on the door.

"Pet..." she said with a lasagna in her arms, which meant either someone had died or been born, as both events were marked with homemade Italian food.

"I need you to bring this up to Mr. Snellack at the end of the street. He's not well, and I've to go to work..." No! This was the best part of the day. No parents, no interruptions, Hercules loaded up on the PlayStation, and the main man himself sitting waiting there, the hanging axes swooshing and clashing in the background.

"Why?" I said.

"Because I'm your mother... and I say so," she said, and that was that.

Mr. Snellack, aka the butterfly man, lived in a house at the end of the street, closest to the wall. In fact, the wall was technically in his garden. I had never considered this fact, which wasn't good considering how often we spent our time lounging about in there.

He had never once given out to us.

There were plenty of neighbors who would chase a young boy out of their garden just for picking berries or kicking a ball into their front yard. Reluctantly, I traipsed to his front door.

The house itself was rundown and dark inside, and there was no car in the driveway which gave the premise an eerie, abandoned feel. I pushed on the doorbell and stepped into the porch.

Through the misty porch windows, the walls were black and grimy, and the carpet looked like a sheep's fleece that had never been washed.

It felt as though the lasagna might rust in my arms, since this whole place seemed to stink of death and decomposition. Even dead, cooked meat in a sugary tomato sauce seemed too alive for this environment, and I wanted to protect the lasagna all of a sudden, to simply chase off back home with it and give it a better end. But I couldn't, as he had come to the door now.

The door opened to reveal a tall man with a cigarette clamped between his teeth and no smile; this must have been the carer, one who did not look very caring.

He looked down at the lasagna, the cigarette dangling from his lips, bits of ash blowing towards the food. "He's inside," the caretaker ordered, still smoking away as I crept beneath the plume of his ashy cloud. His skin looked sick and yellow, the way smokers often do, and he appeared dry and crisp as if he might catch fire from the glow of the cig at any moment.

And to me, it felt as if I was about to go on a horrifying theme park ride, with that sinking in the pit of your stomach before some extreme, death-defying experience. Still, somehow, I managed to put one foot in front of the other, maybe more out of shame or embarrassment of turning back than anything brave or noble.

The living room stank of urine and unwashed body odour, and in the center of the room devoid of entertainment or relief from his condition, was the Butterfly Man.

His body was bloated like an enormous maggot, and his arms twisted around one another, akin to the gnarled roots of an ancient tree. I saw what my mother meant; the way feelers were, it appeared as if his legs and arms were one instead of the separate limbs of healthy people. I was afraid of him, but then he spoke, and that all changed,

"Oh, Ms Thompson really is too kind!" He cooed, and I was surprised by the warmth and candour of his voice that seemed to stand in complete opposition to this body. My mother would have no hesitation in approaching him, I knew; in fact, she would probably hug him and everything. Mum was a born carer, well used to the infirm, whereas I was not.

On the mantelpiece, carefully placed, seemed to be pictures of the invalid as a younger man, in which he wore thick, nerdy glasses like Noam Chomsky, and had a naturally occurring tonsure. He was seated atop a desk at the front of a lecture hall, at ease in front of the rows and rows of students. "Oh," he trilled again, as I placed the lasagna on the table in front of him,

"It reminds me of the streets of Rome, the moon falling on the Piazza, and the sound of clinking wine glasses and the conversation." For the first time, he addressed me directly. "You will thank your mother for me, won't you? I still tell dear Ernie here about the Bolognese she sent me for my birthday." However, *dear Ernie* smoked his cigarette impassively.

"And where are my manners! You must be Deirdre's boy?"

Drool gathered at the corners of his mouth, and shamefully, I hoped he would not ask me to shake his hand. If I touched it, I feared I would be forever cursed, and no soap or shower would ever be strong enough to get the stain off.

He was almost starting to unwrap himself like a snake until he saw my cast.

"Ah, a fellow invalid I see. What happened?"

I was hesitant to tell him the story of falling off his wall in case he got annoyed.

"I fell..." I said, which wasn't a lie.

"Oh, a fall! Well, you are speaking with an expert in falls. I used to fall all the time, off ladders, walls, trees. I was never much good on my feet, but it was great fun nonetheless..."

This was quite a different take from that of my own father who never fell, apparently.

I liked the Butterfly Man, and started to become interested in his surroundings.

I looked to the spot where his TV must have resided. I knew this was the place because there was a clean square, high on the wall, whereas the rest looked black and dusty, or else yellowed. I was reminded of a hotel room on holiday, and of the bedside cupboard from which some light-fingered guest had taken the Gideon Bible with them on checking out.

"I have a TV," I said, telling the truth. "You can have it if you like?" I hoped he wouldn't accept my offer, but that he would appreciate my offering it. But I was not expecting this abrupt response.

"TV? Ha. Good riddance I say," Mr. Snellack said, following my gaze. "I was far too reliant on that thing. Sometimes, losing the most essential thing in the world is the best thing that can happen to you. Why, when I lost the use of my legs, I turned to teaching math."

"I best be going," I said, starting to feel more and more out of place by the moment.

"Oh of course, of course," Mr. Snellack said kindly, though I sensed he was a little hurt. But then again, so was I. I had just offered him my own prized possession and he had snubbed the offer without so much as a thank you. But he did give me a parting gift, in words, without realising.

"Enjoy the falling!"

His eyes were shining like those of a dog about to be taken for a walk.

" Thanks..." I said.

I left Mr. Snellack's house as the evening wore into a stunning pinky purple, dry and dark below the navy clouds which slid in rows like fluffy shuttered blinds. If only I could pull the sky apart and see what was behind it, but I was always below the damn thing. The wall was dark and foreboding in the evening, and I craned my neck again and saw there was a man on it. He stood on a ladder and was little more than a silhouette, still I knew it was Da.

I approached sheepishly from the basin of the cul de sac, the equivalent of a small car park where no one actually parked for fear of neighbourly conflict.

"What are you doing, Da?" I asked, eyeing the ladder half-hopefully. Now, there was an easy way up the top of the wall, a stairway to heaven really.

"Just had to sort this out," he said, and climbed down, taking the ladder under his arm and dragging all my dreams along with it. "This wall has been letting all sorts into this cul de sac for far too long!"

"What did you do?" I asked.

"Just a little security measure."

I could see now in half-light that his hands were black, and he produced a small bottle of a special liquid from his pocket and started to remove the black from his hands.

"What's that?" I asked.

"Oh this," he said, pointing to the tin at his feet, grinning devilishly. "This is paint that never dries. I'd like to see anyone get over that wall now!"

I went home and collapsed in a ball of crippling depression; that was that, then.

The summer went by, slow and uneventful like a lame donkey, and I sank deeper and deeper into my video game abyss. When the winter came, and the trees shed their leaves, it seemed a cruel joke when the doctor finally cut my cast off before the first day back to school; I was robbed of even the fruits of my classmates' sympathy. My arm, newly freed, was yellow and shriveled, felt like someone else's, and smelt like a putrid foot. It was an evil arm.

"It'll be back good as new in a few weeks, but be careful..."

My mum tried to pinch my arm, but this time, I shrugged away.

She made a face. We hadn't been getting along, and that was little surprise since I had been stuck at home, where we got on each other's nerves even more than usual.

"He will be careful with it, Doctor, don't you worry."

I traipsed out into the street alone, to walk home. Stuart had gone to secondary school this year, and so I was the only one out of classes this early in the day.

No-one had been over the wall for the rest of the summer, and even though they didn't say anything, I knew the boys blamed me, because it was my fault for falling off. Also, though they were around, I spent most of my time inside, alone, playing video games.

It was a strange and lonely time, free, but in chains. Success wore the mask of that ten-foot, whitewashed wall which I saw every day of my life, but never seemed farther away.

What hope was there? I was weaker and chubbier than ever, there was paint that never dried on the way, an evil arm, and I had no friends to help and no-one to even prove anything to.

Who would even care if I did climb the wall now?

Maybe only Mr. Snellack.

Dad came home from work in a bad mood, and when I showed him the cast was gone, he barely even registered it; he simply went straight back to fighting with Mom, and I now learned they were getting a divorce. I guessed I wouldn't be learning to climb anytime soon, then.

I left the house to go and kick a ball on the street and I thought about committing suicide for the first time. It just seemed easier than being alive. Things were only going to get worse.

I kicked my football against the curb like a tin can but through the windows of the Butterfly Man's house, a lamp glowed, and I tiptoed to a pillar where I could get a better look inside. There was music muffled by the windows, an old-timey waltz, that strange stepping music that they listened to at balls a million years ago. The Butterfly Man was in his wheelchair, just sitting there, all crumpled up as usual, and his carer was smiling and pushing him in circles.

The Butterfly Man held his arms aloft like an instrument, a human trumpet, which he waved about. Even Ernie was smiling. It must have been the oddest corner of the world at that moment.

I certainly couldn't imagine a place farther from the glitz and glamour of the silver screen, but it was so evident they didn't care. A single light shone on the top of the road, and I thought a car must be coming, but I was wrong. It was the light of a bicycle, someone on a bike.

I stood with my ball under my arm as the sun got closer, and a person dismounted. Stuart. In his new grey school uniform, he looked older, like his brother.

"What are you doing?"

I showed him Ernie and the Butterfly Man, waltzing.

He only laughed, saying, "Are they gay?"

"No," I scowled. "I met him before. Ma sent me there with some food for him, and he's actually alright, you know? Anyway, how was big school?"

"Shit," Stuart said. "Want to..."

"What?"

"I forgot we can't get over the wall. Podge has some fireworks stashed over there."

"And where is Podge?"

"He got suspended and Mam's grounded him." Finally, some good news.

"Can *you* climb the wall?" Stuart said. Well, I didn't want to go home and face the chaos.

Stuart positioned his bicycle at the base of the wall, and I stood from the pedal to the seat,

"Push!" I shouted frantically as I leaped with all my might towards the lip of the wall. I caught a grip, a good grip—not one of those fingertip ones, or a short scrape, but an actual grip.

My evil arm ached but Stuart pushed hard on my arse, and slowly, my hands turned into elbows, and then I landed on my belly and flopped like a seal. Before I knew what was happening, I was lying horizontally on the wall. Uncertainly, I stood up. I'd done it, the highest I'd been in my whole life. I looked down. It wasn't quite little boy heaven, just an overgrown laneway covered in weeds that was dark and frightening. And I didn't want to climb down.

Stuart climbed up next with a big grin on his face. In the dark, he looked just like his Podge. I was sort of afraid of him.

"You did it..."

"Yeah..."

We stood awkwardly beside each other, not really knowing what to say. There was a faint glow from Dublin city on the far-off horizon, and for a moment, we stood and watched, transfixed by the big bad world. The big bad world that was even bigger and badder than the wall at the bottom of Marley Drive. I looked back at Mr. Snellack's house in the dark of the cul-de-sac where his light shone out in the distance.

'Enjoy the falling' I thought, and together, we jumped.

The Whiskey Republic

HARRY SAT ON HIS couch alone. In Portobello, he lived in the downstairs apartment of his mom's house. Still, he had dreams of his own castle estate, a golf course, swimming pool, and a wife who looked as though she belonged on top of a trophy. He was ambitious, Harry, through and through—the best, and he was going to be the best, and that was that, a real Macbeth.

In the morning, he would be starting his first day as an official software engineer at Google! His dream job! The clock was hitting nine-thirty, and Harry was nearly in bed. He could taste the eight hours sleep, and he was ready for it too, raring to hit the sack. Just a quick shower and then lights out. He whistled a military tune as he went to check if the front door was locked, shut, and closed for business, and whether he could safely hit the hay. Outside, he heard a dog barking and the crunching of heavy boots on the stones. Shit!

He peeked through the window, and there on the porch step was a dreadful bedraggled creature, hairy, mangy, smelling like a foot, and next to him was his dog... It was Irish Mike with his overgrown beard and Hawaiian shirt, even though it was approaching winter.

Irish Mike was his best friend and resident bad influence, and he had a sixth or even a seventh sense for when Harry was bored and thirsty for pints. And it was true to say Harry had a dreadful itching for an armpit full of pints. It was something about this new job, a new routine that made him want to scream and run around with his clothes off, but thankfully, he had better self-control than that. But Irish Mike could smell his indecision in the air like a shark with blood in the water, and he would arrive unannounced, with a twelve-pack of Guinness and many stories to make him jealous. That was how he got you; he'd tell you all the mad stuff he'd been up to, and then you had to go out because there was no resisting him!

Booze Hound, Irish Mike's sidekick, was just as bad—maybe even worse. Booze Hound was an Irish wolf hound, once famous for once drinking six pints of Guinness in the Portobello and still walking Mike home after.

He was like a seeing-eye dog, except Mike was blind drunk instead of being blind proper.

Mike was the Irish equivalent of The Dude from The Big Lebowski, laid back and nonchalant, and perpetually high on pints. He was Harry's best mate because he could tell a hell of a story and was the best craic, but Harry's life wasn't about the craic anymore, or so he kept telling himself. In recent years, the obvious gaps between their ambitions were broadening. Harry wanted to conquer the world, while Irish Mike was still enjoying Call of Duty and collecting the dole every Thursday. Harry peered down and saw the twelve-pack of Guinness under Mike's arm. *Oh Lord, give me strength!* Irish Mike knocked on the door three times, and Harry considered not opening up at all. He lingered behind the door, crouched down in his bath towel; maybe Mike would just go away?

"I know you're in there, you prick. I rang your mother!"

"Oh, for fuck's sakes..." Harry was caught rapid. He proceeded to the door.

"Evening, gorgeous," Mike said and gave him a big toothy grin. Booze Hound wagged his tail behind him.

"What do you want?"

"Nice to see you too!" Mike said and tugged at his friend's towel. "What's your little willy doing, locked up in the house all week! Your ma is worried about you? She says you're going soft." Irish Mike nearly whipped the towel right off Harry and left him in the nude in the porch. Harry clutched onto his towel for dear life, and Mike let himself in. Harry was terrified of being naked around anyone, his only weakness, except for pints.

"Why are you here, Mike?" He called after him, "you know I have work? And I can't drink?"

Irish Mike's voice came back, gruff, the hoarse throat of a seasoned drinker.

"Ah c'mon. You only graduated last week, and you've done nothing but hide in the gaff and post pictures of Google and your abs on social media. People are starting to talk..."

"What do you mean?"

"They're say you've gone soft, pal. That you're this gym bro, tech-Google weirdo?"

"Who said that?"

"Me." Irish Mike sat back on the couch with Booze Hound beside him.

"You can't stay, honestly... I have to get up early."

Mike leaned down and opened his can of Guinness with his shiny front teeth like a bunny rabbit's. Harry shuddered. Irish Mike had lost his teeth in a bizarre, drunken accident, while walking home from Wetherspoons on Christmas Eve.

He was so drunk, he couldn't actually remember the details of what happened, but after the dramatic reconstruction, Mike deduced that he must have fallen into a lamppost, teeth first.

He awoke the next day without a drop of blood on him or a tooth in sight—a Christmas miracle. For the last four years, he'd had no front teeth and walked around like a reverse bunny rabbit, insisting new ones were too expensive.

"I guess you don't want the present I got you for your big gay graduation…"

This was where Irish Mike always got ye. Every birthday, graduation, celebration, he was the first one to get you a present. Even your parents would forget before Irish Mike did.

He would emerge out of a mist, bearing gifts, a broad grin plastered on his face.

You could even be holidaying on the island of Fiji, and he'd crawl out of the water with something incredibly thoughtful to whip out of his back pocket, and he'd even have wrapped it up. And it was the same this time. From inside his jacket, he removed a book wrapped in yellow and pink polka dot wrapping. Harry's heart melted a bit.

He unwrapped it: Warren Buffett's autobiography.

"Ah Mike, you shouldn't have."

"Look, I know you're on your way to the top, superstar, so thought I'd pitch in."

"Honestly, that's really nice of you."

"Do you want a can?"

Harry looked at the shower, which was getting farther away, and then back to Mike. It was only half nine; maybe he could just have the *one*? Famous last words. For a person who never made any plans, Mike was always a direct antagonist to any of Harry's. But trying to argue with him was like fighting smoke. Sure enough, sooner or later, you ended up in the 'Whiskey Republic' or some other rusty boozer with the sun coming up and eight glasses of Powers in front of you, with no memory of how or why you got there.

Sometimes, you had to turn into the crash and just minimise the damage.

"Ahh, anywhere but the Republic," Harry said.

Mike pondered.

"What about that new boozer? The one that's full of yuppies like you, who drink craft beers and talk about Apps. What is it, 'Neon Dicks' or something?"

"Neon Lights?"

"Ye the one for all you yuppies; apparently there's a few nice women there though, high society types, might bag myself a sugar mama."

Booze Hound sniffed Mike's sleeve, and he poured a bit of his draft out for him. The booze hound lapped up the foamy brew. Harry very much doubted he was getting a sugar mama; he looked at Warren Buffett and sighed. Maybe in another life?

Outside was October in Ireland, and it was autumn, a perverse mixture of the tail end of summer and the coming winter. Still a weak light in the evenings, but gutters filled with dead leaves and the stars obscured by thick clouds, akin to cigar smoke.

Harry felt awful; leaving his home behind was like a knife wound in his chest. His home promised sleep, and sleep promised work, and work promised success.

At this point, he didn't really want anything else.

They made their way along the Portobello canal where the swans and the geese guarded their newborns carefully amongst the reeds and the silvery water.

Irish Mick started to sing; he had a good singing voice, deep like a baritone:

"*And the auld triangleeee, went jingle-jangleeee, all along the banks of the Royall Cannalll...* Do you ever wonder if swans will become domesticated? Like, when can we have them as pets? That's what I want to know!"

"Who the hell would even want a swan as a pet? Do you know how much food they eat? And they're vicious, you know. You'd wake up in the middle of the night, and they would be pecking the mickey off ye."

"If you had to shag one of them though? The swan would be up there?"

"Honestly, I haven't thought about it much..." Harry snorted and supped on his beer. The conversation had gone quiet, cold even.

"Are you still not working?"

"I'm just going with the flow, doing a little bit here and there."

They walked along the river, which did indeed appear to be flowing, flowing beneath the bridge's darkness up ahead and into the belly of some unknown place.

"Don't you think you should go to college? Get a job? Have a plan?"

"Nah, that's a load of shite. I've got cans, ketamine, and I just prestiged on Call of Duty? Life is sweet. What more do ye want than that?"

"But life goes by quick, Mike," Harry said wisely. "It'll get past ya."

He nodded beneath the canal bridge where there was a homeless man's tent, saying, "That's where it can end up. One minute, you're on top with everything, and the next, nada...Living on the side of the canal!"

"That doesn't look too bad."

Mike started laughing, a deep, husky, breathless laugh.

"What? What is it?" Harry asked, leaning over.

"He's got a bird in there!"

True enough, through the tent's silvery flap net, they could just see two high heels in the air and a big pale arse, bouncing up and down!

"Jesus Christ, the night," Harry said and Irish Mike whistled. "Gowan, ye good thing! See, it's not all bad."

Harry was so sick of Dublin, sick of all the lack of responsibility and the endless brunches and parties. Everything was a big joke. Much like his close friend, he was a millennial, raised in the lap of luxury and breastfed delusions of grandeur. Still, unlike most of his friends who just settled for the internet fantasy, he was on the hunt for his success.

Like Mike, most were just getting by, finding a little corner of somewhere they could hole up and maintain themselves, getting badges of honor in Call of Duty rather than promotions in work. On top of the Portobello Bridge, the orb lanterns cast an orange glow on the dark entrance to 'Neon Lights' rooftop bar. On the balcony, lots of cool high society types were dancing in the disco lights. Harry actually started to feel excited, and a little less guilty.

"Mickey drippers," Mike said at the sight of the two doormen.

"What?" They approached the two doormen. "They won't let me in..."

"No dogs," one said, and the other chimed in, "And no Irish Mikes." Above, on the rooftop, pretty women were dancing, the sound of chatter and cocktail glasses clinking.

"Mike what did you do?"

"I might have gotten caught in the jacks with a couple of ladies of the evening. What can I say?" Irish Mike looked at Harry hopefully. "The Republic?"

Irish Mike considered himself an afficionado of local boozers.

He often talked about starting a reviewing page where he would make up fake reviews for bars in which he got blackout drunk. He called it, 'Forget-the-Reviews.com'.

At least, he would do it if he ever went to any other bars instead of always going to the Whiskey Republic every evening. The Whiskey Republic was a shithole. Your man on the door had no problem with dogs or Irish Mike, as he himself was some sort of war criminal from Yugoslavia who spent more time smoking fags than doing his job, and the corruption went all the way down. They had gone to the Republic ever since school because there, they sold the cheapest pints in South Dublin. You could barely be in the bar five minutes before you'd bump into somebody you knew and have to have some shite conversation.

Harry followed Mike to the bar.

"Two Guinness and two whiskies," Mike said.

"Ah, Mike." Harry swore.

"Relax," Mike said, shrugging his shoulders. "I'm buying."

The bartender poured out two fat cups of Powers.

"That's not what I meant..." Harry said like a truculent child. It was one of those nights in the Republic, with some fifty-year-old auld fella dj-ing and playing nothing but Pitbull and Sean Paul all night long. It was probably the most eclectic mix of people in South Dublin.

You never saw a crowd like the ones the Republic pulled in. It was the cheap pints that did it, bringing in everybody from rowdy students to middle-aged plumbers who filed in after work for the cheap drink and regrettable one-night stands. As the night got going and the drink flowed, the crowd started to mix in unconventional ways.

"Look, I'm not drinking those whiskies. If I drink that, the gloves are off and there's no way I'm getting to work in the morning..."

"Look, there's no way I'm going to stick your moaning all evening unless I get absolutely bladdered. You're not going to miss your big job, ok..."

"I've work tomorrow, and if I drink those, there's no telling what's going to happen. You know what I'm like on whiskey. The last time we drank that, I ended up in the Liffey!"

"Yeah, that was unreal! What's your point?"

"I can't do that now; I work for Google!"

"You mean, you are gay for Google..."

There was a standoff, the two whiskies standing perched there between the two old friends, neither of whom could break the deadlock. Harry looked to the door and thought about just running, turning tail and heading off into the night, then he had an idea.

"I've got a proposition. An agreement of sorts."

"Go on?"

"If I miss work tomorrow because of you, you are never allowed to call up to my house unannounced and kidnap me again. How about it? For all future pints, you have to contact me in writing and get my John Hancock on the dotted line before a drop of alcohol touches these lips..."

"Jesus Christ, Jeff Bezos! D'you want me to fax your secretary while I'm at it? Fine, if you miss your big boy job because of me, I'll leave you alone for good! How does that sound?"

"Delightful."

They shook hands and dropped the whiskey back.

"Michael Douglas's kneecaps!" Harry swore.

"Sylvester Stallone's chin! That's some piss!" Mike started shadowboxing in the air like one of those robot boxers. "I'll get us another round!"

Around and around they went. Harry was now a little bit steamed as the night was wearing on. Irish Mike went up for another, and he scouted out the talent around the bar.

Harry spent his whole life looking at women, but only from afar.

Like a child at a candy store, he was outside the glass all the time, nose pressed up close for a better view. He would never just walk up and talk to them, though, as there was always so much fear, so much chance of rejection and mortification. Because of this, he slugged back a big gulp of his pint and looked around, looking at females but not daring to make eye contact.

"What are you looking at, ye bleedin' predator?" Mike said and planted another whiskey in front of him. Booze Hound sat up hopefully and got a rub on the head for his troubles.

"I haven't had the ride in six months," Harry said, "I think I'm technically an incel now..."

Mike laughed at Harry's unfortunate horniness.

"Jesus, I thought a big corporate boy like yourself, you'd be drowning in women! I've been riding everybody since I got the new teeth put in. Maybe try new teeth yourself...?"

"No way! I don't believe ye. Anyway, I have teeth."

"Well, yep. I pulled a Vietnamese bird outside Mr. Kebab the other night..."

"Mr. International! How though? What's your secret?"

"Well..." Mike had a think and rubbed the hound's head. "I didn't really pull her, to be honest. The Hound here did the work. Yeno, he gets cold, and he starts shivering. So we were on a roll-over there, out from the night before. Three in the morning outside the kebab shop, and the hound, he's shivering away in the freezing cold, and this Vietnamese woman comes up to us. She's young, in her thirties, and crackin'!"

Mike whistled between his teeth.

"She starts, yeno, tearin' up over him, sayin', '*aww, look at him, he so cold. He need to come inside! He need to come inside!*' So, fuck. I'm thinking, alright, I wouldn't mind not being in the freezing cold either, so guess I'll come with him too?"

Mike was in full flow now, all winks and nudges, and Harry couldn't help but get involved. He had a way about him, Mike; there was no doubt. Mike carried on.

"So, I'm sittin' there in this woman's kitchen at three in the morning with a cup of Vietnamese tea and a headful of the devil's dandruff, trying to make conversation, ye know? About what? Exactly! I had to go to the jacks and whack a few bumps into me just to whip up the confidence."

"What do you mean?"

"Try to shift her."

"But like, was it on?"

"What? D'you think I'm taking advantage of her? I'm the one who'd been steamed for forty-eight hours! Well, like ye, I was in her kitchen at three in the morning. So, we were just sitting there looking at each other, her with no English and me talking 300 miles an hour!"

"Sounds awful."

"Yeah, well, anyway, she said no."

"So, it wasn't on?"

Mike shakes his head. "No. You're not listening! She said no *kissing.*"

"No kissing?"

"No kissing, she said only *biting...*"

"What do you mean, *biting*?" Irish Mike leaned over and nibbled on one of his cheeks, but Harry slapped him away.

"What the fuck!"

"That's all she wanted! Who am I to judge? She just wanted me to bite her cheeks, can you believe that? I thought at first it was a religious thing, you know, God and all that, but what we did this weekend wasn't too holy if you catch my drift..."

Harry shook his head. Fuck, he wanted adventures like that.

"You are an absolute dog, Irish Mike; you're living it, man."

"See, I told you? Life's not all stand up, sit down, fold your socks?"

"How did you know I folded my socks?"

"Lucky guess..."

Harry stared over Mike's shoulder at two slightly *older* ladies in the corner, the leftovers of a hen do, probably both in their early forties, late thirties, in great shape with blonde hair, tanned skin, thick black crayon around the eyes, looking like pandas.

One, in particular, was giving Harry a look. He pretended to yawn and flexed in his shirt a bit. She looked like a hairdresser he'd had when he was younger, one he'd always fancied. Just a sheepish wee young fella getting his short back and sides in the mirror, with this woman with her breasts pressed up around his ears. Irish Mike followed his eye line.

"Let's go sit with them?" Irish Mike was a solid wingman when he was steamed, and he had a well-established history of not giving a shite.

"Wait. Please don't..." Harry gripped onto his sleeve, and booze hound barked.

"Why not?"

"I ehh... I dunno, I... just sit down..." Harry was sweating, and Irish Mike took a stool.

"Look what's the worst that can happen?"

"They could laugh in our faces?"

"Then we'll laugh right back! They're wearing pink sashes and willy hats? So who gives a fuck—" Harry took a deep breath. Would he continue being such a coward?

"Ok, but I'm getting some drinks first..."

"Yeowww! This round's on Google!" Irish Mike exclaimed.

There was no art to carrying a tray full of drinks over to a group of women; you just shouldn't drop them and look like a prick. As much as he was irresponsible, lazy, chaotic, and mental, Irish Mike could carry a tray like you wouldn't believe. Cool as a cucumber, he escorted the tray of whiskies, with Harry kinda creeping behind him like his little brother.

"Sorry, ladies," he said, interjecting politely.

They both looked up at him as if he actually worked there and was about to remind them of last orders or something important from behind the bar,

"Did you guys order two sexy young fellas, by any chance?"

He looked back at Harry and nodded while they both rolled their eyes.

"No, fuck off," they said, and Harry nearly did a three-sixty. The hound started barking. The lady turned her back, and Mike nearly fumbled the tray. Harry swooped in and saved the day; this was his job, good cop and drunk cop.

"Sorry about him, ladies; he's had a few today. What my friend meant to say is, maybe would you like a drink?"

"We have a drink..." the more attractive woman said playfully, wafting her hand over the table where, sure enough, their drinks stood mostly untouched.

Harry and Mike looked at one another, and Mike shrugged.

"You could always have another?"

The ladies conferred silently. "I'd agree with that," the more attractive woman said, and the two lads greedily grabbed stools.

Harry stuck out a hand to the lady he was sitting beside, which probably came across as far too formal, given the circumstances.

She shook his hand carefully and with great theatrics, as if he was slow.

"Harry," he said.

"Sharon," she replied.

"Sharon, what a beautiful name. Is that French?" Mike said, and Harry elbowed him in the ribs.

"Stay in your lane..."

Mike turned to the other woman.

"Barbera."

"Irish Mike."

"What's your dog's name?" Barbera asked.

"That's the fearless Booze Hound."

"Why Booze Hound?"

"Cause he's a hound for the booze!" He poured a bit of Guinness out for the Hound to slurp.

"Is that good for him?"

"Full of iron, apparently…"

Harry made small nervous talk. There was no common ground between them. They hadn't gone to school together, and they didn't know the same people. So, what now?

He could talk about the weather?

Somehow, he had to get the situation moving, and there was only one thing for it! He had to ply himself with as much booze as possible. He nailed a couple of whiskies.

"So, where do you work?" Harry slurred in between sups of another creamy pint of Guinness. At this stage, he'd one in each hand—akimbo Guinnesses.

"A little hairdressers' there in Rathmines. Do you know the one? Dr Barbers?"

Harry nearly choked. "Dr Barbers! Ah yeah, I know it, alright." That was where he used to get his haircut when he went to Mary's. Maybe this was the hairdresser? He was meeting her as an adult? This was some sort of bizarre fantasy; was he caught up in a porno?

"And what do you do yourself?" This was the question he went to school for, why he went to college, studied, and made all those damn Google applications!

"Actually I work for Google…"

"Ohh," she trilled and put her hand on his. "The drinks are on you, in that case! I think we caught two rich ones, Barbera."

Barbera made a face as if to say, *maybe you have.* Irish Mike slurped a drop of Guinness from the Hound's bowl. *Such a child,* Harry thought in his drunken stupor. *How does Mike think he's the pulling machine? It's me!*

"So, are you single?" Harry asked in as casual an offhand way as he could manage, trying to look particularly disinterested.

"I might be. Why, are you interested, Mr. Bigwig?"

"Could be. You're an attractive woman."

"I'm a bit old for you, no?"

"I'm actually thirty," Harry lied. "I have a condition that makes me look twenty-four, very rare, under-diagnosed really..."

"Jaysus, I wish I looked thirty again!"

Here it was, his big moment,

"You don't look a day over twenty-nine, Sharon."

She giggled, like a young schoolgirl. This was actually going pretty well, better than he could have expected. Maybe miracles could happen after all? Maybe all his wound-up tension would be released, and he could finally stop intermittent fasting every day.

Harry's mind, his head, was full of adventure and madness, and all the other things that went through the mind of a drunk boy filled with testosterone. Maybe they would get married and have kids? Perhaps he would be a kept man after tonight, and they would move to Aruba. He'd start a little cocktail bar, and Sharon could give haircuts while Harry worked out spreadsheets in the corner. In a spurt of madness, he took hold of the back of her neck.

He kissed her as passionately as he could, as passionately as Sherlock Holmes solved mysteries, and as passionately as Tom Cruise pursued those impossible missions, or something like that. Who knew? They were drunk. It was all a bit of a state.

Out of the corner of his eye, he saw Mike make eyes at Barbera, as if he might also go in for a kiss. So, she stuffed a cigarette in her mouth and threatened him with her lighter. It was a flat no, then. Before he could open his mouth, the lights came on. And when the lights come on in a bar, it is not a pleasant experience. You can start to see everything in way too high-definition detail, and that's when you start reflecting on your poor decisions.

Rather than do that, instead, he pulled Sharon outside and Barbera came with them, the three waddling like a trio of drunken penguins, Mike and Booze Hound coming in behind them, staggering, veering all over the entrance. The Soviet doorman finished his cigarette, which he had smoked solidly for an eight-hour shift as if his pay depended on it, and let them loose.

Mike and Booze Hound almost tumbled into the street, Mike entirely missing the step down to the pavement. Then, they stumbled along, feet and unsteady paws going this way and that, both using walls to prop themselves upright as if it was a losing battle, as if they stood on the undulating deck of a great liner in a force ten gale.

"We only live around the corner, why not come back to ours?" Sharon suggested to Harry.

"Wait, wait," Harry said, pausing, swaying on the spot. "Can Mike come?"

Sharon shook her blonde hair.

"No, honey," she said, simple as that. That was it, then.

Harry looked back at Mike, who was like a little puppy dog trailing behind him, trying to find its feet. This was it. The test of ultimate loyalty, bros before hoes. He could see that Mike wanted to come or wanted Harry to come with him, but there was no way he was passing this up. He had to cut the umbilical cord, had to be gentle—kind even.

"See you later, *cocksniffer!*" he said, and Mike nodded, adhering strictly to the code, no matter how much it hurt his feelings. Mike headed off across the Portobello Bridge, just a tall, shadowy man and his gangly, wobbly dog with its oddly splaying legs.

They stayed just around the corner from the Portobello, a stretch down from the homeless man's tent, which was shut up and quiet.

"Is this your place?" Harry asked, surprised when they arrived at the house. The apartment looked like an Airbnb or a rental and definitely not a place where anyone actually lived.

"Well, it is for this weekend," she said flirtatiously.

"No but like, in general?" He had an ominous feeling standing at the front of the door, as though someone was watching him.

"What? Are you chicken?" Barbera said. "Afraid you can't handle the two of us?"

"No," Harry said. *Stop being such a sack,* he reminded himself. No more of this taking bubble baths and going to bed at eight o'clock; he was walking on the wild side. He'd ditched Mike, and he could at least get a good story for his troubles.

"Lead the way..." Sharon opened the door, and Barbera took Harry by the arm. The hallway was white and lit by fluorescent lights, aesthetically clean. The flat was the same, clean and devoid of any personal objects, not even a phone charger, or a single apple going soft in the fruit bowl. It looked like your apartment at the end of a holiday after you had packed everything to depart. From one of the cabinets, Sharon whipped out a bottle of Jameson.

"So there is life on this planet," Harry muttered. Barbera lit a cigarette, eyeing him.

He was plainly nervous, and the confidence of the bar was wearing off,

"Can I have one of those?"

"Only if you take your shirt off."

Harry laughed. So, that was the game. Sharon poured three glasses, and he removed his shirt, and Barbera handed him a cigarette.

Sharon was about to hand him a whiskey when she stopped.

"What?" Harry said. "No..."

"There's rules," she said. "Lose the pants." Harry was shy but thought he'd oblige the two older women and removed his jeans.

There he was, standing in his boxers, a fag in one hand, a glass of whiskey in the other, with these two women fawning over him.

"Oh he's so muscular! You must be an athlete! Do they have a gym in Goggle?"

For a second, Harry was enjoying the attention.

He felt like a celebrity, a human trophy, a monument, and he leaned over to kiss Sharon and get proceedings started. Suddenly, though, he stopped. Someone was standing in the doorway. After them, he must have slipped inside... it was a small man in a leather jacket with grey hair, and dark, worried eyes. For a second, Harry thought it might be the homeless man.

"Ehhh..." Harry said, unable to formulate a sentence. Sharon jumped about ten feet away from him while Barbera pulled him onto the couch beside her, onto her lap.

"Who the fuck is this?" the man shouted. "Who the fuck is he, Sharon, and why are you staying in this place? You said you were in Belfast for the weekend?"

"I was, Grant, I was meant to be. You see, we were..."

"Who the fuck is that?" Harry whispered to Barbera.

"That's her husband..."

She said, HER HUSBAND! Harry didn't need to be told twice. He was too drunk to fight or think, so did the only thing he knew how to do, and started running. He took off, leaving all the clothes behind him. Took off, under the jealous husband's arms, and out the front door.

He ran down the canal a bit, until he was far away to realise he was outside in the nip. He was outside in nothing more than his socks and jocks. On a Sunday evening, piss-drunk, this was not good. Work at nine o'clock in the morning was looking pretty far away.

His house keys were back in the flat!

He started to panic, and ran over to the homeless man's tent. Could he steal his clothes?

He could see the homeless pair of them in there, bollock naked out by the canal, through the zip. The police would think this was some kind of dogging site! He threw on the homeless man's jocks which were outside the tent, and kept running. There was only one thing he could do, the last thing he wanted to do, but his only option left.

He approached the front of the apartment in Charlemont. There was a light on in the front room, and he climbed the staircase. This was a bad situation. He'd been snotty with Mike all night, for years even, never treated him properly, never given him respect when all he wanted was to be friends. Now he needed a friend, now he was outside in the cold, would Mike understand? Take pity on him? Harry probably wouldn't if the situation were reversed.

He was looking for any excuse to turn his back on Mike.

So, he had to gamble that his friend was a *real* friend and would forgive him.

He rang the doorbell. This was a lot ruder than what Mike had done to him. Ringing the doorbell of his parents' flat at one in the morning in the nip, the shoe was truly on the other foot, except Harry was in his socks. Mike shuffled to the front door in a kimono, a cigar between his new front teeth, and a can of Guinness in his hand.

"Wow, wow, is it my birthday? I don't remember ordering a stripper?" He laughed.

"Mike, Mike, it's all gone tits up, and I need your help..."

Harry was nervously jigging around on the spot; this was the big moment.

"Can I come in?"

Mike looked at him, bollock naked, pathetic, vulnerable as a young baby, and no longer the Billy big balls who, just hours before, had scorned him,

"Ye of course! Stall in. D'you want a can?" Harry heaved a sigh of relief.

"Thank fuck," he said and took the can from Mike.

Harry sat on the couch with Mike and told him the story. Mike whistled.

"I honestly think he was going to murder me."

"So selfish of him," Mike said, "good story, though."

"Look, I'm sorry for bailing on you, Mike. I guess I just wanted to do something mental and felt like you'd understand."

"Yeah, always, brother. I know you're a big dope. Sure, we all are..."

"Yeah, I think I get that now too..." Mike wasn't too concerned.

"And yeah, I thought about what you were saying, and I probably do need to get my act together at some stage. I just love the session? I mean, I'm an absolute animal? What can I say?"

"Too true; you are a bleedin' weapon."

"But that's why I got the new teeth in. Saved up my work money, figured I'd shape up a bit yeno?"

Harry laughed. "That's progress, aye, who knows what'll happen?"

"I fuckin' know what'll happen. You're going to work at nine in the morning, bud! Bed for you now after you finish your can."

"I think I've had enough..."

Booze Hound rolled over on his back on the carpet below them, and Harry reached down to scratch his belly.

"I wouldn't do that if I were you."

"What, why?"

It was already too late, and the Hound let loose a powerful Guinness fart that curled the eyebrows of both the lads.

"Jesus Christ!" Irish Mike exclaimed. "We need to get that dog off the drink..."

Uncle Bob's Van

WHAT WOULD YOU DO if everything had gone to shit? The spare tyre is gone, the sun is beating down on you, no food in your belly, no-one will help you because you are in France and the battery is dead? Oddly specific situation, I know, but this is the position I and my father found ourselves in, right smack dab in the middle of France, at the end of July, and the epicenter of a global pandemic. How did this story start? How did we get here?

Well, it started as it meant to go on, tragically.

Uncle Bob died while travelling around the South of France in his van. Bob loved travelling. Every summer, he'd pack up in his home-made van and head off to France, Germany, and Spain. He was an eclectic and gentle soul with a passion for Bob Marley—the reason why we called him Bob—and playing spontaneous DJ gigs to make friends with the locals.

He spent the winter in Dublin tinkering with his machines, and the other six months testing the wheels out. Delayed this year by the coronavirus, he had just managed to get away by two weeks when he unexpectedly passed away. We were all understandably shocked. There was the question of who would go over for his things and finalise his return to Ireland?

I knew my Dad would volunteer, and as I said to him, 'if you need anything.' The last time my Da had seen Bob was before he left, when Bob came to stay with him and work on the van. The two brothers, aged just fifteen months apart, hung out for a couple days, talking, eating, and walking the dogs up in the Dublin mountains.

It almost broke my heart when I saw the tears well up in the old fella's eyes as he recounted those precious moments they spent together that last weekend in Dublin. There was something very sentimental about the old rust bucket, and we had to get it home.

We sat in the Hatter Cafe in Dublin, ketchup and fry stains on our plates and cups of milky tea, while outside the window, the rain was pouring down—heavy, like a monsoon.

"I'm going over to get it," Da said, "I'm leaving on Saturday." He'd always gone the extra mile for me. Even if I was in Spain, he always said he was twenty minutes away, and I believed him. He wouldn't ask me to go with him, nor did he need me, but I figured with a crazy mission like this to go to the South of France and reclaim his dead brother's busted-up van, he could use some backup. Sure, what were sons for? So, of course, I said I'd go with him.

Call it a sixth or even seventh sense, but I knew this would be a wild one.

Little did I know that the actual events would exceed my imagination a hundredfold. Things would go more wrong than I could ever have conceived.

Still, we were all in, and in the words of the Blues Brothers, 'We're on a mission from God'. It was decided. I was heading to Montpellier.

From square one, obstacles started to befall my journey. The bus broke down on the way to Dublin Airport on the motorway side, which just never happened—except, it did. I thought nothing of it. A spare would be along shortly; that wasn't my responsibility.

Other passengers got upset, pouted, and complained, but I stayed cool. I was the monk, patient, could watch a blade of grass grow for twenty years, or so I thought. It was a seven a.m. flight, and there was much fussing over masks, boarding passes, and the logistics of travelling across a foreign country by train, boat, and van. Google maps—what's happening?

We were flying to a place called Carcassonne in the South of France, a medieval town with a walled city and high turreted castles as in a fairy tale. We had to get from there to a police station in Bédarieux to collect his belongings and the van, and then the real fun began. A ten-hour drive across France from the south to the north's tip, and a ferry journey back home aboard the W.B. Yeats. The big problem we faced was getting the van actually going; despite it being searched by the French police, no-one had managed to find the key.

Da insisted that he knew Bob, that Bob would have hidden the key, and that Da could think the way he would when he was sick and find the keys. That's right; we were going to Sherlock Holmes it. This wasn't much to go on, but goddammit, it was good enough for me. If we didn't find the keys, our mission was over even before it had begun, and we'd have to get a flight home with our tail between our legs. To get from Carcassonne, we had to take a bus and two trains, taking approximately three hours. Then, we had to arrive at the police station between two and six o'clock when they were open. The next day was a Sunday and the following day a bank holiday, so we really had to be there before six o'clock. No, we really did.

Two-hours-and-a-half-hours of sweaty, crooked-neck sleep on a Ryanair flight, and we were in the Languedoc. When we deboarded, I pulled the mask down to let my nostrils sample the fresh foreign air, inhaling the hot, sandy smell of holidays that I never expected to have in 2020 in corona's age. That alone felt like a small victory.

We went through passport control and Dad nodded at the police officer's gun,

"No magazine..." he said. I often wondered how the old man's eyes worked, how he saw things like this. Sure enough, when I peered around, the magazine was missing from the officer's gun.

"Just for decoration?" I suggested.

"Or so no-one can take it..." An interesting thought.

I and my Dad were chalk and cheese. He was more disagreeable, the warrior, rough and ready for conflict, and for any challenge or complaint.

I was the diplomat, the planner, ever the customer service agent, agreeable and ready to work things out, but together, there were no two better bucks at your backs in a struggle, despite our different managerial styles. We could fight, talk shite and write you a screenplay like you wouldn't believe; nothing could stop us, this was the American dream in action.

So naturally, right from the airplane, our problems continued.

We walked out cool as two cucumbers, immediately missing the 11 a.m. bus to the Gare du Carcassonne while being so cool. I'd heard bad things about midday in France and not getting anything done, but I assumed since this was an airport and not a third-world country, we could get some service; well, it turned out I was wrong. The woman behind the desk said a taxi was impossible to find and another bus would be along shortly, and left on her lunch break.

The bus never arrived. When the next shift came on, they explained that it would be at three o'clock and not twelve. So, we had wasted an hour for nothing. The old man was biting his lip, gesticulating, pointing to the sign above their heads,

"Oh, pardon me! I didn't realise this was the misinformation desk!" he said.

Safe to say we ordered a taxi.

I was determined not to log a complaint right out of the gate. Fresh off a week of customer servicing, I had all those angry customers still in my head. I couldn't become one, and I wouldn't, not yet. We waited an hour for the taxi to show up, by then it was now nearly two o'clock in the day, and we still had to travel three hours across Montpellier to reach the police station on time, and couldn't be late. We ordered another taxi to replace the first that had never even appeared and finally, we were on our way to the Gare du Carcassonne.

The streets were white and sandy, a lazy cafe and a beautiful place for a holiday along a green canal. Still, we had no room to breathe. The watch on my wrist felt as heavy as an anchor. The train station was a big yellow building, like an old saloon with a clock in the middle of its forehead. Great. Another clock. We paid the taxi man and went inside. There, we saw two beautiful French ladies behind the counter who had to deal with my pass-leaving-cert French.

"Je suis un retard," was about the height of it, and there was much confusion.

"Easy, tiger," the old man said. After much sweating and translation, we learned the train was full and that there wasn't another until half past three. We ran back outside in time to see our taxi man departing and just about managed to flag down another.

"How much to Bédarieux?" Da pointed at his notepad, where he had written down the name. The taxi driver took out a calculator—not even on his phone, but an actual calculator—

which is always a bad sign.

"250 euros..." he said. We exhaled deeply, but what choice did we have? If we missed six o'clock, then au revoir! So far, our bill comprised the flights, taxi and two croque monsieurs in the airport, nearly five hundred quid.

The van, on the other hand, was probably worth six hundred quid.

The French police in Bédarieux were actually quite sound. There were communication issues, of course, but we got the job done, got Bob's stuff, and saw his ID cards and laptop. Finally, I was glad we had made the trip.

One of the police officers then agreed to take us from the station to the van's lockdown. He was a funny officer and drove while speaking on two phones.

"Zis ees very illegal," he explained in his French accent. We said we wouldn't tout, and I think he appreciated that.

He took us to where the lock-up was, down a dusty lane with a big steel shutter and filled with decommissioned vehicles. Beyond this shutter, I got my first look at the van, packed into a corner, rusted and slightly in bits. Now, we just had to find the feckin' key.

The police officer explained that the French police had searched the van for *one* hour and found nothing…The only thing we had to go on was Da's theory that he could channel Bob's mind and find the key. After forty minutes of searching in the sweat-soaked heat, I was really starting to doubt his psychic abilities. I remember saying the phrase, 'needle in a haystack', and we were juiced. The van's inside was like something you wouldn't believe, a mad scientist's lab on wheels, bits of power steering, wires, insulation, blocks of wood, butter, DJ equipment, booze, machines I'd never seen in my whole life.

Da was a mechanic, so he'd say, *oh yeah, that's such and such for a clutch. Oh yeah, that's a spare radiator.* Bob could have been building a UFO for all I knew. We took everything out, then we put it back in, and we took everything out, and we put it back in.

I whispered a prayer to Saint Anthony and asked God to return the keys to us.

If he did, I said I'd be a good wee lad. Bob knew how everything worked. He had rigged the whole thing up. He had five batteries in the van, solar panels, and he was the only one who knew how everything worked and where everything was. We were fecked. On top of that, the place was a mess after the police search, with gone off ham, onions, and butter on the floor. Honestly, I just stopped thinking about the key and started cleaning, scooping butter up off the floor, trying to get some order because it was complete chaos!

So I was there, top off, trying to scoop this melted butter in the hot French sun when I noticed the lid of a box in the middle of the floor with some wires.

Listerine mouthwash, and a funnel in it. Everyday objects.

I lifted the lid to throw it out of the way so I could actually see the floor, and good fucking lord, there it was, right in the center of the carpet: A PAIR OF KEYS.

Holy son of a beach!

I jumped out of the van like a man who had just won the Sam Maguire cup,

"FECCCKING RIGGGHT!" I shouted, and Da cheered.

"I'm glad you're my son!" he said, which oddly was sort of life-affirming.

We were in business, thunderbirds were go. Buzzing, we washed the oil from our hands and the sweat from our brows and got a jump-start from the garage man, who was just happy to be rid of us; the engine came to life and started chugging. We were in business, as long as the engine didn't conk out and we had to jump the thing again...

We headed for the local Carrefour for some Sambos and sparkling water to celebrate. I was in charge of plotting a route. Only then, looking at Google maps and trying to plot ferry routes from France to Dublin, did it dawn on me what sort of trip we'd actually departed on. In Montpellier, we were in the very South of France, and the only ferry you could get to Ireland was on the opposite side of the country, Cherbourg or Calais.

I don't know why I thought we could get one there and just sail around Spain!

We would have to drive the whole of France in this van that you couldn't risk turning off, or we wouldn't be able to start it again. To say I began to get worried would be understating it.

We booked a ferry for the next day, heading from Cherbourg to Rosslare at three o'clock in the afternoon; we would then have to get a drive from Rosslare back to Dublin.

It was approaching six o'clock in the evening, and the journey would take ten hours. Surely, that was more than enough time? Wasn't it? We wouldn't miss the ferry, would we?

I mean, there was no way we'd miss the ferry? Was there?

At least we had a trajectory, a plan, a goal, and a route in front of us.

We whacked on Bob's tunes, which he listened to as he drove around, some cool blues, and took off on the open road. We travelled by carefully planning out everything, measuring times, angles, and Da was cool as a cucumber.

I was terrified of missing that Ferry but Da's attitude was, *whatever happens, happens.*

"Don't worry about the things you can't control," he said, and so we drove three hours of the journey, over mountains, hills, along motorways and through stunning sunsets.

The scenery was incredible, and Da pointed out that Bob must have really loved and enjoyed the beautiful countryside scenery on his journey. He mentioned that the philosopher, Krishnamurti had once said, *the moment you look at a stunning piece of scenic beauty, the mind completely stops in awe of the vision nature has presented to you, and in this very moment when the mind stops, this is true meditation.*

Whereas I—*I* was just thinking about the boat!

That night, we got a hostel room at the Ibis, with no air conditioning; your man did us a solid and charged us full price.

We got some grub in the local steak house, and prepared to arise at five a.m. where the real journey would begin, the Sunday of all Sundays.

Why were these things always on a Sunday?

I didn't sleep so well, and the mattress was made of plastic.

I was farting like a trooper, and what with all the disturbances, five a.m. rolled around quicker than expected, and I awoke with the words of Marcus Aurelius in my mind:

Man was not made to stay in bed.

So, I arose from my slumber. You know things are fecked when you think your phone has been charging all night, and arise to see there is only twenty percent battery left. Not ideal. The first problem we encountered after that was starting the van. We had to jump it since the battery was dead in the front. As I mentioned before, there were five batteries, but only one was still working. And the only reason this one was still working was because it was attached to a solar panel above the driver and passenger seat, absorbing the sun.

As it had been night and everything, we assumed we might have trouble with the solar panels. We had nine hours for a six-hour journey, surely enough? But who knew what might go wrong with this van which had been parked up and done more miles than I'd ever seen on anything? We managed to jump the van, and the engine started chugging. The sound of that engine coming alive each time was like the sweetest music you could ever imagine. Except this time, there was another sound along with it, a high-pitched buzzing, like an alarm for a door open. Except, when you opened and closed the doors, it kept on going.

"That'll drive us mad," Dad said, I shrugged.

"What choice do we have?" I replied and whacked the tunes up to try and cover it.

After about three hours, we reached the middle of France, the intersection between North and South. There's a big complex of petrol stations there, and we went in for a pain au chocolat and a couple of al-pacinos, throwing on our balaclavas—well, our masks—and leaving the van running. We threw all the organic rubbish in the van in the bin on the way, and things were looking up. When we returned to the van after the feed, I even realised that the buzzing sound was coming from the solar panel control board.

And I pushed a button, and it stopped: *alrigghhtt!*

High fives all around, but little did I know I'd completely screwed us in the long run...

Back on the road, Bob Marley was blaring. It was approaching eleven o'clock with a three-hour journey ahead and over four hours to do it in! Tight, but barring any obstacles, do-able.

We were raring along on the motorway, one-thirty kph, in the old rust bucket van, satnav leading the way. My Google maps were supporting, and the battery was just holding up.

It seemed that finally, the stars were aligned, and if we just kept this up, then we'd make the ferry and everything would be fine.

Suddenly, there was a loud bang from the front, right-hand side of the car.

"What was that?" I said.

"I think a bird flew into the van..." Da said.

"That was a tyre, that was definitely the tyre!"

"No way..."

"Fucccckkkkk!"

We pulled onto the motorway's hard shoulder, at the entrance to a field of hay with a big electricity pylon in it, only to find the goddamned tyre had exploded.

To be fair, at that speed, we were lucky the thing didn't flip, but the tyre was shredded to bits and would not be driven on again. I looked at my watch and ran the calculations. If we could change the tyre in thirty minutes and get back on the road, we still had a shot of getting the ferry. But the real question was, could we do it?

Oh my God.

You've never seen anything like it.

First, we needed to find the tools—remember those keys?—Well, everything was even more mixed up now than that time after us, and the Gendarmes had wrecked poor Bob's van, and time was running out. We dug everything out of the van, and I was lying there underneath the bed, trying to pull out tools, a mouth full of dust and insulation hair. We get a socket set, a hammer, and an old toolbox my Da had made when he was fifteen. We found the spare tyre under the van, but Bob had welded it on so no-one could steal it!

Cars whizzed by us at one-fifty kph while we tried to hit the wheel off with a hammer. So, I was under the van, exhaust pipe in my face, trying to raise the tyre off the latch.

Trying with a socket to get bolts off, sweating, I felt as though I'd lost a couple of kilos at this point, and I'd eaten nothing since five a.m. but a single, solitary, measly pain au chocolat.

I left Dad with the tyre because we needed to find the jack to lift the car. Again, impossible. I then took everything out of the van twice, exhausted, calling up every resource and bit of endurance I had left. I'd found the keys, so I could find this jack!

But no. I couldn't.

We passed the half-hour mark at this point, and I knew we were going to miss the ferry. But still, my brain was telling me that maybe by some miracle, we could still get there. A delay? A cancellation? Man overboard? Anything. Dad had got the tyre off now, and we were both working our way through the van for the millionth time, searching, rummaging, raising this, looking under that, feeling here, running our hands there.

We had everything out on the motorway, strewn before us like a vehicle parts jumble sale: solar panels; wood; insulation; tools; everything. All fear of the speeding, bullet-like cars that whizzed by our ears was gone, even if they were close enough to trim our ear hairs.

We shimmied relentlessly in and out of the van. In, out, in out. Door open, door shut.

We took everything out, put everything back, took everything out, put everything back.

In, out, in, out. Then, just when we'd finished, we tried again, attempting to put it back in a different order! As if that would help... How could he not have a jack!

He *must* have a jack, driving all day.

Surely to God, that arsehole knew that old tyre was bound to go at some point? So, why the fuck did it have to be now? Why now? We took out the bed and literally threw it out of the van.

And right there, lurking, skulking there beneath the sink, I spotted something, what I thought was a bit of wood panelling, but was actually another cupboard!

Boom, boom, boom, I opened the door and pulled out the jack!

Two for two, baby! Alrighhhht! Back in the game.

Only one problem now: I was about as much use as a chocolate teapot for changing a tyre.

So, I was basically assisting Da, the same way I did when I was eight, handing him tools, measuring socket wrenches, and hoping they were the right size.

The jack was a car jack and this was a massive van, so Da had to do some wangling and manoeuvring to get it lifted. Very dangerous. It kept slipping off and almost squishing Da.

This was one hell of a mission, but somehow—against the odds—the old dog got it done! Lesser men would have quit, but we were not those lesser men, and persevered.

We finally jumped back in the van after an hour of sweat, and nearly tears.

I recalculated.

So, now, we had four hours to go and only three hours to do it.

Well, we were fucked—but as before, maybe, just maybe, if still we went on... It was worth a shot, wasn't it? The new tyre was a good one, and we were back to ripping up the motorway at one-thirty again in no time, only now, the engine started overheating.

The light flashed up on the dashboard, next to another circle symbol that had been lit the whole time, but which we did not recognise.

"We need to stop her. She won't make it at this pace. We need to pull off!"

At this point, my phone ran out of battery, and we were now reliant on the trusty satnav for directions, and everything was going to shit. Maybe at this point, I had some naive fantasy we could pull it out of the bag, but the toll bridge killed that dream; the queue of traffic was half a mile long and moving at a snail's pace.

I looked out the window at the coarse grass of the fields.

We weren't getting a ferry today. Fuck it.

We made it to the top of the queue after about twenty minutes, and because the van was a right-hand drive, I was in charge of the toll bridge payments. And—well, you could just predict it—the machine was fucked. I was sweating so much, thinking about missing the ferry, and every time I put the ticket in, it just popped out of another ticket slot like a game of whack-a-mole. Oh, for the love of Christ. I was poking the ticket, in, out, pressing buttons, sweating, swearing, and it just kept coming back out. Here we were again then, playing the in-out game.

In—out. In—and out.

This was some perverse game of hokey-cokey, for feck's sake.

"I think it's broken! It must be broken!" We went to get moving again, and then the van cut out. But now, the ticket went in, and the ticket *didn't* come out.

This time, the light turned green. I swiped the card to pay the twenty-seven quid, and yahoo! For a moment, I didn't realise what had even happened, then I remembered...

We could only start the van with jump cables, and here we were, sitting at a toll bridge with a mile-long queue of traffic behind us.

"Fuccccckkkkkk," the ignition whined, as if even the van knew it was screwed.

I jumped out of the back of the van and started pushing, while Dad steered her, and for the second time in an hour, we were on the hard shoulder of the same motorway!

The ferry had well and truly been missed at this point. The 550 quid were gone, and even worse, the van was now toasted, and the jumper cables wouldn't work. I was sun-stroked, fatigued, and I'd still only had a pain au chocolat all day. We tried calling to the motorway security, but they were French and wouldn't help us. The battery we had been using to jump-start the car was now inexplicably dead, and so we went around, testing all the other batteries in the car, finding all of them dead. Dad came up with a plan to perform battery surgery right then and there on the motorway side, a kind of CPR for knackered vehicles, but I was losing faith. *Why won't he give up and call the AA? We've failed, and this is the end,* I think.

I was staring at the battery, defeated. All I could think of was that it was like that scene in Pineapple Express when they spent all night in the woods and came back to the car battery being dead. "What do you mean, the battery's dead?"

"It's dead, ceased to exist! No longer living! Defunct, demised, kaput!"

Then I just started pushing buttons, and realised what had happened—the beeping sound. When I'd turned off the beeping sound, I had killed off the solar panel controller.

Now that was back on, but of course, how long did a solar panel take to charge?

We could be out there for hours!

We'd no water, no food, and this place was stinking hot. This was when I learned truly that the endurance test only really started when you had no endurance left. Everything else had just been foreplay up until this point, and now we were in the big leagues.

After about an hour at the side of the toll bridge with an endless stream of cars driving past, we decided to try and jump the car one last time. Maybe, just maybe, we'd be lucky; it couldn't hurt. The battery level was 10.8 volts, while all the others were only eight. Maybe, just maybe... and sure enough, the engine roared back into life. *Hallelujah!*

Except now, we had missed the ferry, and the van had turned into that milk truck from Father Ted that couldn't slow down. And we couldn't turn it off, and couldn't keep going because the engine was overheating.

We were surrounded on all sides... but look, at least we were moving for a change.

We pulled into a gas station and let the van idle for a while. I drank a Yop and tried to calm the hell down. There was a moment when the car was being filled with diesel, and I was being filled with Yop, and we became one, man and machine.

I remembered the words, *don't worry about the things you can't control,* and was so sickened we had missed the ferry, but we still had to get home. We were still three hours and forty-seven minutes away from Cherbourg, and the funny thing was we would continue to be three hours and forty-seven minutes away from Cherbourg for the next five hours.

As I mentioned, my phone had run out of battery before the toll bridge.

The satnav hadn't been updated since 2008, and it was not the most reliable piece of equipment in any case. I had been using Google maps to keep a handle on it, but now we were thoroughly in the satnav's hands. Unfortunately. We set off back on the route again.

Obviously, we missed a turn off for Paris, which we were supposed to take, so instead of finding another turn-off, the satnav rerouted us back down the motorway.

Neither of us noticed. We just kept going.

We soon passed through another toll bridge and that gave us a ticket, which was strange, but I also thought nothing of it. I only started to worry when we returned to the same toll bridge after another ten minutes, where we had been broken down for the last hour. The machine asked for the ticket. I did what I had done last time and just put the ticket in, except this time, instead of twenty-seven quid, the charge was £106.50. Fuckkkkkkk!

We'd just lost 550 quid on the ferry, plus the taxi, and everything else. Now we would have to pay another hundred quid for turning around on the motorway? No way, no how. This was it. I pressed the assistance button, and I pressed it again. And then again, like a demented patient in hospital, desperate to be brought a pan to take a shit in. Well, I was irate by now.

I was going to make a complaint. I was!

I leaned out of the van window, and could see myself in the side view mirror, sunburnt, covered in dirt and oil. I must have looked like a lunatic to them, and at this point, I was one.

"There's been a mistake. Look, we aren't paying this, we just came here ten minutes ago and turned around..."

"You have to pay for it, I cannot cancel..."

"We want to make a complaint! We want to speak to a manager!"

"No, no, no." And they leave us sitting there.

Da hadn't a bother in the world. He'd sit there all day, he said, if that was what it took.

I was having images of the gendarmes rolling up, taking us to prison. Really.

At least, with our luck, that's what would happen.

Ending up in prison was the next logical step in this tragic story.

"Da, can we go..." I said plaintively, my voice sounding as if I might start crying at any second, weeping like a baby into its sleeve. I was feeling like a kid again, but Da only smiled.

"Are you breaking, lad?"

"I can't keep doing this! I'm tired! I'm fed up." He shrugged.

"Daniel McGrath," he said. "I never thought I'd see the day. Pay them then..."

I'd tried to pay the fee, but the card got rejected.

Now we really couldn't pay, and we couldn't leave either!

"We can't pay! We can't pay!"

A toll bridge worker came out, and meandered to the side of the van, huffing and puffing and sighing with exasperation.

"Turn off the engine. Turn off the engine!" she shouted.

"We can't! We can't!" I shouted back.

"You are Eenglish?"

"Irish, we're *fucking* Irish!"

We had to show our passports.

"Oh, ok…" she said and printed us off a bill, which had to be paid in twelve days. All I can say for legal reasons about that is, feck French toll bridges.

Just say nothing and keep saying it.

So they let us go, and the satnav started bringing us the same way again. Seven hells, we couldn't go back to the toll bridge, we agreed. Head there a third time, and we were definitely ending up in some French prison. Da and I would be out there on the toll bridge, battering some French customer service agents—probably with a car jack!

Not how this mission was supposed to go. We would have to re-route the satnav to 'no-toll roads'. Now, we were three hours and forty-seven minutes away from Cherbourg again, which changed to six hours with our new directions. *Country roads, take us home!*

The tension was so great that I realised I hadn't pissed since five a.m. that morning, and I still didn't need to. You would think the worst was behind us, that Bob's van would behave from here on out, and yet this was when our greatest challenge yet came about.

The brakes went!

That little circly illuminated light was the brake pad warning, and every time Dad used the brakes, there was this dreadful metallic screech, the metal of the fucked brake pad linings pressing up against the metal of the brake discs. We were going through country towns the whole way, and I didn't know why this was, but apparently, every French town had at least two roundabouts. Didn't matter how tiny it was, those two roundabouts were sure to be there.

To save what little was left of the brakes, Da was using the handbrake, and so we were drifting around roundabouts in this twenty-foot van like a giant schooner drifting at sea.

At every roundabout, there was a near-death moment when some other car was coming around, and if we missed our drift even slightly, we would blow directly into the front of it. After a while, I stopped caring. I had metamorphosed into a younger version of Da.

Can't control something? Then screw it.

That was the solution, and one that covered all eventualities in life.

So, our lives were in Da's hands now, and the best I could do was keep a lookout. We were getting to Cherbourg, or we would die trying. We were in a box, with no spare time. Couldn't start the van, couldn't stop the van either. What was there to worry about except keeping going?

We'd handled every problem so far. No matter what, I felt we'd handle anything else that befell us. I was sure I knew how Columbus and Michelin and those other great explorers of the past felt, worn out but determined. The first advertisements for the D-Day museum heralded our arrival at Cherbourg, after an extended fifteen-hour journey.

The irony of us landing on the D-Day beaches the wrong way around was not lost on me. I felt like a soldier from the trenches, reflecting a lot on men and machines, and on how difficult the human enterprise had been, and the challenges our ancestors had faced and survived.

△▽△

Cherbourg was a bit of a heap, an industrial and port town without much else going on.

We tried another Ibis hotel, but this was entirely booked up.

The satnav route down to the ports was a long and winding, downhill road, which didn't make us feel too confident. The brakes were scrap now, as if they didn't work anymore, and we needed at least three or four hundred meters to stop the thing. Apparently, this was precisely how the old motor cars—the very first ones—stopped. They had no form of brakes, so you just had to hope for a soft landing at the bottom of each hill.

That was Da and I's precarious position in this thing, each time we encountered even the mildest of downhill routes, trying to predict ahead which way to steer it for the least damage to ourselves. Anyway, we checked into a pretty sketchy B&B and spent another evening in the Buffalo Grill, eating greasy food and guzzling sparkling water.

The ferries were few and far between, and it was a bank holiday Monday, to top it all.

The only ferry that day was scheduled for 16:30, arriving in Dublin at 10:20 the following day. We had no choice, but this time, we weren't going to book online, and instead, we would go to the ports directly to see if Bob had booked a return journey for him and the van.

Dad also wanted to get the brakes done, but I put my foot down; we were not missing another ferry, and we would get there, even if we had to leave the van in the parking lot.

The next day, the bank holiday Monday, we made our way to the port, slowly, inching along the mountain road. We were apprehensive to say the least. The country roads had been quiet, but this was a town, and the reality of our braking situation was if a car stopped in front of us, then we were going into the back of them. We inched along the long, winding, mountain road to the city, hoping to God that we wouldn't end up behind anything else.

Thankfully, because of the bank holiday, it was quiet. But still, the journey was nail-biting stuff. When we came to the final furlong, a roundabout with a turn-off into the ports, I thought there was some humorous irony that in the center of the roundabout was a statue of the Goddess Athena, the Goddess of Wisdom, and we nearly drove straight over her.

The van tipped to the side as we bumped around, and thank feck it was so heavy, or we would have flipped. In Irish Ferries, we'd got a ferry booked for that same day, and they took pity on us and gave us a 100 quid discount, bringing our second ferry bill to another 553 quid… In total, the trip cost almost £2000, and the van was probably worth £600, at best.

As Da said in the car park while we were anxiously planning how to ascend the ramp onto the ferry without sliding backward and killing somebody, "You'd wonder what it was all about?" But we both knew what it was all about, why we had endured such a beating, travelled in such arduous conditions, and never stopped moving forward: it was for love.

Love for Bob, love for Da, love for our family.

We got on board the ship just about, and I spent the evening on the deck, watching the sunset from the W.B. Yeats, the fishing boats bobbing on the horizon in the distance.

It had been about doing something impossible just to prove you could, and I only had one wish left—that there was an afterlife, and Bob had got a chance to see us two eejits bringing his van back home, because he would have got some laughs out of that.

Milltown Cemetery

JUST AS THE JURY had before them, the parole board sat across from me, their eyes scrutinising my conscience, searching for signs of a *murderer.*

"Why do you think you're eligible for release, Thomas?"

"Because I've learned my lesson…" I said to the man in the middle of the parole board with the fat neck and the red face. "That's why."

"Well, I've heard that a lot," he said, stubbornly.

"I'm not lyin', though…"

"You might not be, but how do *I* know you're not lyin'? What do I have to go on?"

He was as tough as an old tree root, experienced with criminals in the North of Ireland, with those of us scarred by the troubles and left behind in the system.

"I'll tell you the story," I said, "and you'll believe me".

The truth was I had been rehabilitated before prison, before court, before sentencing, everything. The time I had to do was a formality because I had always known what I'd done was wrong. I had never met Anthony Horner, a Nationalist boy from the Falls in West Belfast, but I learned later that he'd been a sweet boy who loved football, and wasn't tough but never a coward. He had just been in the wrong place at the wrong time, exactly like all the other young fellas before him, just as I had been too, though on the Loyalist side...

He had never had any chance of winning. You see, there were four of us and we had knives, so it was easy and we carved him up like a turkey. He was cheeky, said things he shouldn't have, and that's why we poked him full of holes. His father had to watch the videos in the police station, where we were surrounding him like crows and tearing his son apart.

We didn't see Anthony the same way we saw each other, though. He was a toy, a Catholic teddy bear for us to take our anger out on; such is the young's cruelty. This is the story of Anthony's father and of how I came to know him after murdering his son.

△▽△

Anthony's father, Joe, visited his own father after Anthony's funeral in City Hospital, Belfast. His knuckles were white, gripping onto the edge of his seat. No man should have to bury his son, and the thoughts of revenge were already consuming him.

Joe was by no means a soft man, and he had as we say in the North, *a history*.

"I'm gonna get every last one of them, Da. Hunt them down like dogs, do one after another and then disappear, Da; I have no choice now."

His father, Bugs as he was known, was a big man, but the cancer had withered him away like a grape in the sun. He wore a white hospital gown and an IV pumped his food into his veins. There was not much left for him after Joe's mam had died, and they'd expected him to go along to her soon enough. He'd had a hard life, Bugs; growing up in working-class Belfast and raising nine kids was no cakewalk, and if there was one person who should have a chip on his shoulder, he was the one. Bugs was tough and scrappy.

There was a famous story about him in the West, too, about when he'd gone to collect his boys from school, and a British soldier called him a paddy.

"You're a big man, saying that with your gun," Bugs told him. "Put it down, and I'll teach you a lesson, son." So Joe and his older brother Conor left school and came up the road to see their Da having fair digs with a soldier from Liverpool while a crowd of school kids looked on, cheering. There were riots that night in Ballymurphy, but he maintained it was worth it.

"Son," he said light as a breeze, as the cancer had made him weaker than Joe ever imagined.

"If you go after those boys, you may dig a grave for yourself. There's some things you don't walk away from."

"What do you mean, Da? So, I just let it go? Let those savages live after they took the life of my boy?"

"You're not God. You don't decide who lives or dies, none of us do."

"We've all decided who lives or dies, Da, you included…"

"And look where that got us? Half can't even look themselves in the mirror, and the other half are dead. I've lived long enough to see the wheel go, boy."

"Da I've nothing left. Maura's broken down in a fit, we're falling apart, so what else is there? We could have peace!"

"There is no peace for some things, and trying to stop the hurt will only make it worse."

Joe's father had had these fits, seizures.

He would seize and almost levitate off the bed. It was eerie to watch; you wouldn't think the old man had that kind of strength in him, but it came from somewhere. Joe made his living as an electrician, and there was a thing electricians knew, which was that when you were electrocuted, it wasn't the charge that sent you flying. It was your own body. The sudden switching on of every cell, every muscle, and every ligament, all at once like a light switch, turned you into a human projectile. Joe accepted there were many things in life he did not understand, and why I killed his son could not be one of them.

Joe put his hand on his father's.

"I shouldn't be upsetting you like this..."

"You might as well take me out the back and shoot me, like one of the dogs."

"I don't think I've enough ammo, Da..." His father laughed and coughed, and he beckoned Joe in for a hug.

"Remember, son, some things can't be undone, and revenge isn't as sweet as everyone imagines." Joe nodded, then he thought about Anthony, how in his final moments, he had called out for his daddy. But Daddy had been nowhere to be found. He had to live with that, his failure as a father to protect his son. At least revenge was a victory of a kind, a way to even the score.

"God forgives, son. Go see the priest."

"God won't forgive what I'm going to do..."

It was mid-July in Belfast, and the weather was warm for a change.

For a few moments, Joe forgot about his son and the gang of murderous youths. Joe had been born in Belfast and bred from the West, where there had been no shortage of conflict, riots, bombs, and the British soldiers. Joe got out, escaped, and only returned when he married a woman from South Belfast who had never been involved in anything.

His older brother, Conor, had gone further in his early military career, you could say.

Joe sat down at a little tea shop on the Falls Road next to the Milltown Cemetery. Over the low stone wall, Joe saw row after row of headstones planted like sunflowers. On a day like today, death didn't look so bad, and more like a picnic, lying out in the sun on the grass all day.

Funny how they call them plots, he thought—grave plots.

Joe ordered a cappuccino. He wasn't feeling hungry. The waitress carried out a tray and placed it in front of him. He lifted the mug, appreciating the warmth between his fingertips.

"Our Joey," a familiar rasping voice said. Joe recognised his brother but only faintly. He hadn't seen him for many years and they only ever met up when somebody died. He wore a mismatch of sporting gear, a brownish fleece, and a woolly hat, even though it was roasting outside. He had a lopsided smile, apologetic like that of an awkward teen, and he carried his shoulder as if a rifle were slung over it. Everywhere he went, people lowered their heads respectfully to him.

"Conor," Joe said and hugged him, as they always did,

"Good to see ye... How are ye?"

Conor fixed him with his pale blue eyes and said, "Aye not bad, but more importantly, how are you?"

"Aye, aye..." Joe said, taking his hand, "I've been better..."

The brothers had not spoken for a time.

Not out of any grudge, but because life had just taken them separate ways.

There were seven others, but meetings were often sporadic and unplanned. When they'd been younger, Joe was always the idealist, full of plans and dreams of the Republic. Yet Conor, who didn't care half as much, had paid the price, and now he was haunted.

Just looking into his eyes, you could see the ghosts. Conor had been locked up and served twenty years for the attempted murder of a British soldier. Still, after he got out, Conor just wanted a normal life, where others would have wanted revenge, Joe included.

"My condolences. Anthony was a great wee fella..." Conor said, and apologised with a tilt of his head. "It's a damn shame. Are you looking into it?"

In other places, this could have meant anything. The funeral? A flower arrangement? The church? But in Belfast, it meant something different.

"I haven't decided," Joe admitted and let his head fall an inch.

"I can have a word?"

"No, I wouldn't hang anyone else for it."

Conor shook his head. "Do they know it's sectarian?" Joe said truthfully.

"Conor it's always sectarian. Why do you think they've not arrested him yet? We all know where he is? What's stopping them?" Joe eyed his phone warily.

He had read that the police could record conversations through a smartphone even if the thing was turned off. Conor caught his eye line.

"Just don't do anything rash, I know what you're like." Joe nodded. Conor reached into his coat pocket, as if going to remove a gun, and Joe almost flinched. In Conor's hand was an envelope, a mass card, which he handed to him.

"If you need anything, you know where I am," Conor said and hugged his brother again.

"Aye, aye, thank ye..."

"And tell Maura I said hello..."

"I don't know if that's such a good idea"

"Oh aye, she still bitter?"

"As a lemon, kid."

"Can't win 'em all."

"And will you get some Vitamin C or something? You look like you're see-through?" Conor laughed, and for a moment, they were reminded of when they were brothers, fighting over t-shirts, grub, having the craic.

"Aye, and you ease off those fish suppers, or we'll have another death in the family."

"Ye wee bollix…" Conor stood up, and the black mountain loomed over his shoulders. He always looked chilly, even in the warm sun.

"Be careful tonight." He was right; tonight was the 11th of July, and Joe had forgotten.

Joe felt like saying something more to his brother, but he didn't.

Words had a way of coming back to bite you in the hole.

In front of the cemetery was a black car, and in the car was Joe's wife, Maura. Maura was from the South. She was still dressed in black with two mascara streams on her cheeks, and her blonde hair a lighter shade of white than he remembered. He knocked on the glass gently, and she got out reluctantly. There had been little communication between them since the murder, except the speech she had given him that morning. She told him not to speak but to think, knowing what Joe was going to do and that she couldn't be a party to it. She often thought he was a stubborn git, and Joe thought his wife was a pushover. Still, he took her hand in his as they walked through the graveyard towards their son. Funny how he still thought of him as his son. Joe couldn't even bring himself to have Anthony cremated because he felt as if was losing something, as though there was still something of Anthony left in the buried body.

Milltown cemetery was a Catholic burial ground at the foot of the black mountain, where the field of tombstones stretched out as far as the eye could see on the rising hills.

Joe felt Maura's hand become loose in his and pull away.

The graves of the wealthier folks towered over the paltry ones; even in death, there was competition, failure, and success. "Seems sad all we leave is two dates and a name. Makes you wonder what all the fuss is about."

"*We* remember Joe, not the stones."

"The stone lasts a lot longer, love."

"When I woke up this morning, you were an electrician. When did you become a philosopher?"

"Since you asked me to start thinking..."

Did they bury murderers, Joe wondered? Did they get the last rites? How many men in this cemetery had taken lives for a righteous cause and gave their lives all the same? The fight had to be, and yet the consequences were nearly impossible to live with. They were up to their knees in bodies, just as we were, and Joe had been interned in the Maze for a week.

The soldiers pressed a hot radiator to his legs, the barrel of a rifle against his neck. They tried to force Joe to sign a confession, and Conor signed instead.

If it hadn't been for his older brother, he would have done twenty years as well.

He shuddered.

Anthony was buried in the back where the newer bodies were brought.

Bobby Sands was buried there, the victims of the Ballymurphy massacre and it had been the scene of the 1988 attack by loyalist Michael Stone during some Catholic funerals. A sad reminder of the injustice and vengeance that was part of Ireland's history, part of Joe's history.

Joe was happy because his boy's grave was at the back and not a part of the historical exhibition. They passed a couple of older women and busy, warm dogs, and gave out friendly nods. Finally, Maura asked the question she had been thinking.

"Have you thought about what I said?"

She was the picture of a widow, beaten down, wrinkled like a tissue. They both blamed themselves, though for different reasons.

"I have..." Joe replied.

"And what have you decided?"

"I can't let this slide, Maura, it's not like someone slashed my tyres, or robbed the wheelie bin. They've killed our son, for Christ's sake!" They reached Anthony's grave, a little rectangle of black marble with his name, date of birth, and death date.

Joe had inscribed 'beloved son' for an extra five hundred quid, but what was the point? What was the point of anything but his revenge?

"Killing them won't bring him back. It'll be you in there next to him."

He hated her *harbinger of doom* routine, like a black raven, a signpost on the way to the grave. She didn't know what he was capable of.

"I've no intention of dying, Maura..."

Suddenly, she took hold of him. She was pressed close, and he was nervous about whether the dog walkers saw how strangely his wife was acting.

"I'm leaving, then," she said. "If you don't get over this, I am going because I won't be part of it. I won't be a part of *any* of this. I don't know how you do things up here, but I won't be a part of the murder of any more kids..."

"Alright calm down. Stop making a fuss."

There was a man nearby, watching. Middle-aged, bald, and with a tiny white brush moustache like an English serviceman. From him, Joe felt the same kind of sadness that radiated from himself, as if today might be the last day on earth for them both. He worried the man might look at him. He worried if they made eye contact, he would burst into tears.

Joe watched the loyalist bonfires' tall skeletons around Belfast as they drove home, a plan forming in his mind. He sat in his chair when they got in and opened a bottle of whiskey.

He turned on the TV, not watching but wondering how many other sad sacks in Belfast were planted in front of the box tonight, nursing wounded souls, too scared to stray outside or down the street on which they lived. Trapped in the house like cats. Joe always hated the night of the 11th, and when they were younger, they always went on holidays, fled to Donegal or the South. In nearby East Belfast, he could hear the drummers practicing.

The bonfires would soon be lit, and the whole place would descend into hell, like the purge. No-one could stick it, with gangs of feral youths, assaulting people, stabbings, shootings, parades, Union Jacks. For us loyalists, it was a holiday, like Paddy's Day, for them. I was building the bonfire with my mates, putting up the last Irish flags to be burned and some of Gerry Adams' election posters, not knowing I was on a collision course with fate.

In Joe's house, the evening wore on, and when Joe was just getting sleepy, the house phone rang. One of those house phones with the cable attached to the wall so you had to stand up to speak into the thing. There was a nervous voice on the line.

"Mr. Horner, you better come by this evening. Your father's taken a turn for the worst, and we fear this could be...Well, you should probably come in. Thanks." His father was in City Hospital, high up, in the palliative care ward. Joe didn't wake Maura, as he would go in by himself. He reached into his pocket for his keys, and instead gripped the card which Conor had given him. Inside the envelope was a mass card with a little stained-glass Saint Patrick on the front. He decided not to drive, and instead left by foot, too drunk to take the car.

If he did, he'd be arrested for certain on a night like this evening. He was last to arrive because he had walked.

The room was already full of siblings, brothers, sisters, and then cousins and aunts, and uncles and neighbours. Bugs was a popular man. Conor was there, characteristically cool and unfazed, even around death. He hugged his brother and went about hugging the others, too.

They didn't see each other much, but he loved all of them.

There wasn't much strength in the old man, they said.

They gathered around the bedside as the old man convulsed and shook.

The hospital had specially sent for a Catholic priest, and he came to his father's bedside in no awful rush, a hunchbacked priest in his black suit, with a turkey neck. He spoke some words that none of them could understand and made peace in ways they couldn't see.

"I'm going to your mother, son..." His father whispered and held onto Joe's hand.

His father seemed calmed by the arrival of the priest, and his breathing slowed. It was almost as if God was allowing him this passing moment, between worlds, just to be with his family. The priest said more prayers and held the rosary beads above his head.

Joe realised it had been nearly thirty years since he last prayed, and the words felt strange on his lips, though he still remembered them.

"Our Father in heaven, hallowed be your name. Your kingdom come, your will be done, on Earth as it is in heaven. Give us this day our daily bread, and forgive us our debts, as we also have forgiven our debtors. And lead us not into temptation, but deliver us from evil."

Joe didn't believe in heaven or hell or God, but he did feel that his father deserved some peace. He was not a perfect man by any stretch of the imagination and had been harsh at times, but he was a man, and he had suffered and sacrificed for them. They were all alive, weren't they? He looked around the room at his family's faces; sure enough, they had come this far.

If there was forgiveness in the world, he wanted his father to have it.

He wondered if this was hypocrisy, if he could want forgiveness for someone but had none himself? He was glad God had to do the forgiving, because he would not know where to begin; all or nothing, maybe that was the truth? He spent some time with his family, drinking tea from plastic cups and telling all Bugs' stories. He told them about the fight with the soldier, which most had forgotten except Conor, who remembered their mother scolding their father afterwards, as though he was one of the boys. Joe had sobered up and regretted leaving his car behind him now. He and Conor traipsed out into the car park together, the sounds of fireworks and screams piercing the night sky.

"I'll give you a lift?" Conor said. "You don't want to be walking around this evening."

"I'm not going home, Conor."

"I'll take ye," Conor said, resolute. Joe looked at his brother. He might condemn the both of them? But Conor wasn't leaving him go.

"Fine," he said, "but you stay in the car."

They drove through the city that was full of smoke and fire and gangs of youths.

"How did you do it, Conor?" Joe asked. "How did you forgive them?"

Conor shrugged,

"I didn't. I wanted to live my life, that's about it. They owned me in prison and if I hated them, they'd own me outside as well. God keeps the score, not us..."

"How did you ever forgive me? I shot at him, not you."

"No Joe." Conor said, "that never bothered me, you were younger. I knew you just needed a second chance."

In my little corner of Donegall Pass, the bonfire was forty feet high, and the Union Jack flew from every lamppost on the street. Everybody was out on their bottles of frosty jacks and cans of Heineken. The Irish flag on top of the bonfire had melted, and we cheered. I had always hated the Fenians; I didn't know any, but I knew they loved the Pope and the IRA, and I hated them. Mam and Da and everyone else I knew hated them too.

I don't know if you'd classify this as a stable home life, where over our front door, the Union Jack flew twelve months a year. Ever since the fight, I'd been very popular, as if I was in the gang, but I didn't feel like myself anymore. There was a lot of guilt I had to ignore.

I wasn't born to kill, and when I heard the young fella had died, there was a part of me that couldn't stomach the truth; I was wrestling with that conscience.

I cleared my throat.

In the courtroom, the members of the parole board were bearing down on me. One tapped his pencil. Were they even listening to me? Did it matter? I felt the anguish leaving my soul,

"I was outside in my house's front garden, playing with a little Staffy pit bull, and I played with his head, ruffling his ears back and forth, letting him bite me; he was too small to cause any real damage. The peelers were never around on the eleventh; they wouldn't dare interrupt the bonfire to do as we pleased. From my front step, I watched the flaming tower, the smoke blowing up to heaven like the tower of Babel. Then the dog started growling, and there was a man in the darkness at the side of the garden. This was Anthony Horner's father, Joe.

"Usually, when a person appears like that, locked on, it's bad news. I was half expecting to get blown away. Then when I didn't, I thought he was a drunk who'd had too much in one of the pubs and was trying to find his way home. I wasn't particularly brave on my own and had no plans to take him on, but he was looking straight at me.

"Fuck are you looking at?" I said,

"I'm looking at you," he said. "Are you Thomas?"

"Who's askin'?" I searched around for my own parents, but he was blocking them, over his shoulders, I could only see the head of the bonfire, and he was cast in shadows.

"Don't act all shy."

"What do you want?" Finding the courage to speak. I had no relation to feelings or anything like that. I knew happy and angry and not much in between.

There was just a queer look on his face, and his features sank as if something was weighing down on his head, and when he was done wrestling with whatever it was, he said, "I have to forgive you. I'm not allowed to choose. God says to forgive, and maybe I don't know any better." He gestured to the bonfire, the flag. "I know you are a child, like Anthony, like I was. There are demons in the world, demons which take hold of a person's mind. I blame those demons. I just ask that when all this is over, you do something with your life, and you do it because you took my sons."

He climbed over the gate and took hold of me in a tight hug, the tightest hug I'd ever gotten, tighter than I'd ever been hugged by my own father.

I broke down.

I broke down because this was Anthony Horner's father, and that must have been how Anthony felt, how much he was loved by his father. And I had taken him away. I sniffled in front of the jury and judge. Seems stupid, but in a way, I felt as though he was my dad, as if I had let him down. "I can't give him back to you," I told him.

"Then do something with your life," he replied, "I'll never forget that. Do something with your life because you took my boys away from him…"

Love & Moustaches

BARRY SPOONED SOGGY CORNFLAKES into his mouth in the hopes his wife would stop talking to him.

She was standing about six feet away, her hands on her hips, and he felt his chances were slim to none.

"Well, what is it then?" she demanded. "I'd really like to know..."

Her peroxide blonde hair was silver in the weak light of the kitchen, her once tanned skin pale and dulled. Barry swallowed his mouthful of soggy cornflakes.

"Can we not do this now? I'm about to go running..."

"You are always about to go running," Karen said. Barry was dressed head to toe in Lycra running gear. He wore a pair of glare-resistant glasses, which he moved to his forehead so he could actually see his wife, Karen.

"It's a complicated question, Karen," he said.

"It is not a complicated question, Barry," she said. "You're just gonna give a complicated answer..."

"I just haven't had time to think, ok?"

"Well, I don't know how you spend your time then, Barry, because it certainly isn't with me or your son..."

Barry let the spoon sink into the cereal and put his hands behind his head. He'd had no time to think about anything; between his business, his running, and his twenty-three-year-old Filipina girlfriend, he was incredibly busy. His life was the busiest life it'd ever been.

"There are variables," he said.

"Like what?" she asked.

"Like, is it how I love myself or how I love you?" he answered.

"Love is love. It's the same thing..."

"No, I love hot dogs, surely you are not the same as hot dogs?" he asked.

"That's because that's not love for other people is it? What about support, caring for another person?"

"We've been through this, dearest. Sympathy solves nothing..."

Barry furrowed his brow, and one foot started to tap the ground beneath the glass table. He was running late; now his run would be delayed and then he would get to the office later which meant less time for the affair. Things were getting away from him.

"This is just the hormones, darling; this pregnancy is making you depressed..."

"I'm not depressed. I just have an unsupportive husband who can't bear to look at me anymore."

"You haven't been taking care of yourself, and that's the first sign of something wrong..."

"Oh, here we go..." she said, and she crossed her arms.

Barry leaned forward onto the table and cocked his eye.

"Go on, take a good look," she said, "it's still there..."

Barry exhaled.

"Are we ever gonna get past this?" She asked.

Karen pointed to her top lip where, unseen from the distance at which Barry sat, four hairs had been growing for the last twelve months into a moustache. This timeline was coincidentally when

Barry had started having his affair. He had looked at these hairs in a moment of weakness.

Barry hoped his wife would deal with his discomfort if he just made her a little embarrassed, but in fact, quite the opposite had happened; there was a stand-off.

"You can love me with it or not at all, Barry!"

"I do love you. It's just a matter of..."

The moustache she had been attempting to cultivate for the previous months was a constant source of tension in their relationship. Barry was attracted to Karen, but something about the moustache made his blood run cold. He felt it was him, or the 'tache.

"Self-care, Karen? That's a kind of love? Or concern about being attractive to others..."

"Maybe if you had made me feel attractive for one day since we were married..."

"There was our wedding night?" he muttered, and she wrinkled her nose at him.

"Yes, when you got so drunk, your best man had to carry you to bed."

"It was lovely before then..." Barry had been raised by his grandparents and his mother. He remembered sitting at the kitchen table at his grandparents' sixtieth wedding anniversary. His granny had kind of looked like a dragon with her wrinkled, leathery skin and marble green eyes. And he'd asked her how she and grandad had made such a good marriage?

Her lines curled up in confusion.

"I don't really know," she said, "You just get on with it, don't you?"

Barry looked at his mother. "You're lucky you didn't marry one like me!" she said. Then after that, she hurled, "Men are pigs..."

"You're a hippy who thinks we should all just lie in the grass having picnics all day, and you think I'm some 1950's conservative man who wears a three-piece suit to bed!"

"I only treat you that way because you act that way..." Karen said.

"That's who I am! I'm not acting, I'm not like you. How is this any different? You're criticizing who I am, for criticizing who you are?" He rubbed his ginger beard with an open hand. "We're just different..."

"You said you weren't attracted to me anymore! You said I had a moustache!" she cried.

"A Ronnie."

"What?"

"I said you have a Ronnie, not a moustache..." Barry put his hands in the air.

"A Ronnie is a moustache."

"A Ronnie is what you get before you have a moustache... You are not quite there yet."

Karen nearly shrieked in frustration.

"You said you don't find me attractive!"

"Ok, so if I stopped shaving my face until I looked like Osama bin Laden, you'd still love me?"

" I'd support you..."

"I wouldn't want you to support me because I'd have gone mad!"

"So, you think I've gone mad?" She pointed to the corner of her lip where three dark hairs grew out of sight. "So, you think I am growing this Ronnie to spite you out of my madness?"

"I just I can't... it's not the hair. It's what it represents!"

Barry shook his head, and she nodded.

"And what does the hair represent?"

Barry didn't know, that was the truth, he didn't know what the hair represented. But whatever it was, that indefinable symbol just out of the reach of his mind, it made his hair stand on end. He was much more comfortable with the twenty-three-year-old Filipino dance instructor who had about as much body hair as a dolphin.

Karen brushed one strand of hair out of her face before crossing her arms again.

"Everything we do is a statement," he said. "We communicate with our bodies, and you leaving that Ronnie there is saying you don't give a fuck anymore."

She kept her arms crossed.

"Well, maybe I don't…Maybe women are made to feel bad about how they look when this is how we *actually* look? And you just can't handle it because you are a little baby boy still… and can't handle a real woman."

Barry was furious. He closed his eyes and pretended to be blind. He lifted a vase from a plinth next to the dinner table and waltzed it around the kitchen in his arms.

"Oh, my dear, you're so great, so wonderful! What did I ever do to deserve such a cold, clay woman?"

"You're a prick…"

He paused. He *was* a prick, and he'd always been a prick but if he was being honest, that didn't bother him one bit.

"So, that's your definition of love then, me being ok with your moustache?"

"And yours is a waxed upper lip?"

Her hands fell to her hips, akimbo. Barry threw his in the air.

"So what? You'll just keep growing this moustache forever as long as we're married, and I'll just keep pretending I can't see it on your face until it hits the floor?"

"If I shave it off, it'll grow back darker!"

Barry slapped his forehead with his open hand.

"We Googled it. That's a myth…"

"*You* Googled it and then printed out this page on 'how to shave your Ronnie' as though you were handing me the fucking Bible!"

"You want support and encouragement? That's my offer. You're trying to improve me right now!"

"This is different..."

"That's a double standard...You think I don't know what love is!" Barry said this last sentence to the drapes above a small kitchen window which was misted in a process he did not understand. He didn't know why the glassmakers did it; probably so people couldn't see in, but then you couldn't see out either. He knew love.

He'd loved plenty of women, hundreds, maybe every woman who had even existed.

"Maybe I don't know what love is?" he said to his wife, 'Or maybe it's because I just don't love you."

The room went silent, completely devoid of sound. Nothing moved, and a pin would have sounded like a train driving through the front door. Barry fell very still.

"You don't what?"

"I don't love you. I thought I did, but I was wrong. These things happen. No big deal..."

"Barry, stop playing. You married me, and I'm carrying your baby, our son. And you don't love me?"

Barry paused. "Yeah, yeah," he said, "just a bad joke..."

He stood up and came closer to her. "You know I love you." He pulled on his glare-resistant glasses which made him look like a big fly. In the blue neon mess, she could see herself, warped into a cartoon character, and she could taste the soggy cornflakes on her husband's lips.

A Great Big Chimp

"HE'S A MURDERER," MRS. Garvey whispered to her secretary. This giggly, precocious, young girl had just started working there. "Don't be acting so damned excited...".

"It is kind of exciting, though, don't you think, Mrs? We'll be in the newspaper."

Mrs. Garvey turned a paler shade of white and put a hand on her pregnant belly.

In her mid-forties, she wore round, moon-like spectacles on her hook nose and vaguely resembled an owl, if you looked at her only briefly.

"Not in the slightest..." She said it so harshly, the young girl scuttled out of her office.

Mrs. Garvey had a harder stomach when she was younger, she thought. For Mrs. Garvey, the more children she had and the older she got, the more frightening she found the specimens who came into her office. Mrs. Garvey was the only clinical psychologist in Co Fermanagh who specialised in psych evaluations of the criminally insane. Truth be told, she didn't often have cases like this one: a triple homicide. Today was not business as usual.

Most of the time, she had people pretending to be crazy to get a lighter sentence or avoid heavy jail time. Still, today, she had a man who she believed must be insane and yet wanted to be tried as competent; why? She thought, what did he hope to achieve?

She had read through his file carefully. He was an oddball who lived out in the Aroo woods by himself, a farmer by trade. He used to mix well enough in the town but was no stranger to a barroom brawl or two. He had money and invested heavily in the infrastructure, which gave him a decent name in the village; he built these roads and all that.

He only ever went to primary school, like many farmers, and never travelled farther than ten miles from his house. He'd lived alone in the woods for most of his life, but had married in recent years and had two children with his wife, and they were three and five.

Emphasis on *had.*

Through the door they brought him. Mr. Chimpy, he was called. He was short, fat, with a brownish farmer's tan and no more than three silver hairs on his head. He looked like a melted action figure, the sort you'd see holed up in the corner of a bar, not speaking to anyone. He looked apologetic, weak even, but you could see the blackness of a shark in his eyes. The two guards deposited him in her office, without her even getting up.

"We'll be just outside, Mrs., if you need us."

"Thank ye, lads," Mrs. Garvey said.

She called everyone lads, since they were all boys to her.

They closed the door behind them, which they weren't supposed to do.

She was a big lady, a mother of eight, and had been around and seen everything a child could offer. She was in her forties now, and patience was wearing thin with her own younglings. Her youngest, Craig—who, especially since Conor McGregor came on the scene, had been nursing dreams of becoming a cage fighter—was proving to be her latest bout.

Over my dead body were her exact words when she left. The thought of broken bones, pain, fighting; no way. Her husband was no use, of course, and he took the boy's side, as always. Sometimes, she felt completely alone in the house, as if no-one was there to support her.

"Mr. Chimpy, how are you today? I hope you are not too warm?" She was always the mother, always fussing over everybody, even this murderer.

"No," he said, shifting uncomfortably in his seat. Outside the window, Garrison town's grey narrow strip, a post office, a Spar, a pub, and a church, stood whitened in the sunlight. Mr. Chimpy was used to the outdoors, while indoors was always too warm for him no matter the temperature. He breathed through his nose, a slight whistle in his nostrils that did nothing to bother him but drove everyone around him mad.

"So Mr. Chimpy, let's get down to brass tacks. I'm to find out if you're mad or not..."

"I'm not," he said and chewed his lip. "Everybody talks in this town, yet nobody knows a goddamned thing!"

"You mean they're mistaken about the fact you've killed your family?"

Mrs. Garvey had a way of babying everyone, and Mr. Chimpy was most certainly not the babying type. He fixed his black eyes on her.

"No, Mrs.," he said, "I did that, but what choice did I have? We were going to lose the farm, and she was leaving with the kids."

"So you killed them?"

"Well, they'd be dead without me, anyway." On her page, Mrs. Garvey made a little X and wrote down beside it in her neat and looping handwriting, *cogent*.

Mr. Chimpy had dark black rings around his eyes, and his teeth were half-rotted, and there was stubble on his neck; he looked like living excrement.

The thought of how he looked probably didn't occur to Mr. Chimpy, perhaps because he didn't consider other people to be real, a key trait of psychopathy. Her own husband was also a farmer, an ordinary working man. Sometimes, he bought her flowers. He never wore a suit and tie, yet he was a saint compared to the man who sat in front of her.

"And do you feel any remorse?"

"My only remorse is that I did not go with them. I lacked the courage to do that..." She was taken aback but made sure not to display any emotion; often, men like this thought she was weak, doubly so with the pregnancy.

"Why didn't you kill yourself? You killed everyone else." She removed the file which she had spent all of last night reading, unfortunately. Drugging, strangulation, burning the bodies.

"I had to be punished for what I'd done."

"Why?" He whistled through his nostrils as he inhaled.

"Do you read, Mrs?

"No, I'm listening..."

"No, do you READ"

"Oh yes. Yes, I do, why?"

"I never learned, but I remember in schooling, they used to tell us this story about the Greeks, that old fella who ate the kids for being too loud in the evening..."

"I think you mean Kronos, a Titan who ate the other gods so they wouldn't take over from him?" She was basically a buff on ancient Greece and Egypt, mostly because all of her kids loved those stories, the old ones, the classics as they were called. They'd sit down engrossed for hours with them. But where the hell was this middle-aged farmer's head?

"It was the kindest thing for me to do. What was out there but suffering? Pain? And death? I've seen enough of life to know that's all there is."

"So that's why you killed him? Out of mercy?" Her face felt a little flushed, and she wanted to open the window but was afraid to move. She remembered that on the wall behind her was a photograph of her and her children right in front of Mr. Chimpy's black eyes. She wanted to say all manner of things, prostrate him, and scold him, but that wasn't her job; she was there to discern fact from fiction, myth from reality.

"You've kids?"

"Yes?"

"You love them?" She had to laugh, nervously.

"Of course, I love them."

"Then how can you let them live? Knowing that people will break their hearts, that they could be run over by tractors, cars, get cancer, die in a hospital bed?" With a note of desperation in his voice, he said, "Is it not better to go unexpectedly in the night? When you've been loved all your life?" She struggled to speak and cleared her throat.

"Well that's what happens, that's life..."

"Life is cruel," he said. "We have no right to create it, and we should have stopped a long time ago." She shuffled her file, shameful of the emotion in her voice.

"When I was young, I wished my father had dared to do what I did," he went on. "Just end things for us instead of letting us live all those wasted years, all that pain and horror, through all of his drinking, his cruelty... Better to just finish us off dead, and of course, when my mother left him, things only got worse. She went mad, and there was no rest, and then I was married, and I thought now? *Now* there will be a break from the pain? But no, like the tide, the pain always returned."

She felt sick and the baby kicked on her stomach like a little hand knocking on a door.

"But do you not feel any...guilt?" she asked him.

Mr. Chimpy thought… oh, he thought.

She could see he was rooting around in whatever went on inside his head, whatever software he had that she didn't. There were temperaments, and the sociopathic and psychopathic all had the same character. For the most part, they were 'disagreeable'. The real question was, why? Why would anyone *end* up that way? Or did they begin that way in the first place?

"I felt a release," Mr. Chimpy said, "I felt as if I had done the holiest thing of my entire life, that I had finally done God's work. I had saved them from the worst fate imaginable: being alive. Did you ever watch the Discovery Channel? You see those monkeys, the great big black ones with the little eyes that stare out in the night?"

"Chimpanzees?" Mrs. Garvey had, in her more romantic youth, been a fan of Jane Goodall. She liked the idea of a strong woman going out to live in the wild with the primitive creatures, understanding them, civilising them.

"They murder, kill, eat the other little monkeys. Catch him in the bush, still alive, screaming and OM!" He bit down on an imaginary monkey with his rotten teeth, and shrugged,

"No feelings, no cares, and even they are not as cruel as us human beings."

He shifted uncomfortably in the seat.

"Are you sure you aren't too warm?" she said, and got up to open the window.

His eyes followed her pregnant belly. She realised that beneath the desk, he wouldn't have seen it, but now he couldn't take his eyes off it.

"I'm six months along," she said. He watched her stomach like a tiger through a cage.

She had a horrific vision of him leaping across the room, tearing the foetus from the uterus and eating it right there in front of her, but still she wouldn't give in to her fear.

This was not his office; this was *her* office.

A crazy idea, a mad idea flitted into her mind. She wanted to see what he would do?

"Did you ever feel them kick? Like they are swimming in there or yawning, maybe waking up?" He couldn't take his eyes off her bump. She wanted to see what he would do.

"Do you want to touch it?"

She held her belly there, forward, daring him. Mr. Chimpy raised his mucky hand with the silver manacles on his wrists. He put a hand on the stomach, and horrific flashes of him ripping out the baby flashed through her mind, images in which she pulled away.

But instead, boldly, she stood there.

He looked away.

"No," he said, and made no bones about it. Mrs. Garvey cleared her nostrils and sat down. She made a note on her piece of paper and looked through the office window at the nosy young girl still trying to catch a peek of the monster who was just a sad, weak man; she would learn, Mrs. Garvey thought, *we all do, sooner or later.* Mr. Chimpy was taken away and Mrs. Garvey loitered at the end of her day at the secretary's desk; she seemed surprised to see her.

"How did it go?" she asked.

"He's not crazy anyway, if that's what you mean."

"I don't see how he couldn't be," the secretary said. "He just looked so normal, like somebody you would see in the shops? Or the pub?"

"Evil is not special," Mrs. Garvey said, "we are all more than capable of it, but only the lowest ever achieve its heights..." Mrs. Garvey waited for the secretary, who seemed relieved that someone was going to walk with her outside, into the world which felt far less friendly than before.

How Not to Get Away with Murder

Montana, January 1996

DO I RECANT AND live? Or die a rebel against the system? Decisions. Decisions. Decisions. The press called my crimes the 'most heinous and horrifying acts of the 20th century', which I thought was a bit over the top.

Everyone knew me. My 40,000 word manifesto was published in every magazine in the world, detailing the dehumanising and deleterious nature of the modern technological-industrial complex and the racist, capitalist system, which was viewed over a million times.

I was to stand trial on ten counts of illegally transporting, mailing, and using bombs, and three counts of murder and faced a least consecutive life sentences, at worst, the death penalty.

My court-appointed lawyers were disgusted by me and insisted that I must be insane.

The first one was a lady lawyer, June, first in her class at Harvard, and of a pretty high pedigree. The second, her lackey, was a pencil-pushing weasel who made me sick, an academic just out of law school, who thought he knew everything.

"Look," the female lawyer said.

Oh good, she was going to level with me just like on TV; I hated TV.

"If you don't plead insanity, they are going to give you the chair."
She was right. I was in a real bind. On the one hand, there was a pretty strong case that I was mentally ill. I lived in the Montana woods, alone, making bombs and writing complex manifestos in code no-one could read, but on the other hand, I had a mission. A moral mission! A moral mission to destroy the capitalist system before it was too late! Obviously, admitting I was a deranged madman and not mentally competent to stand trial would damage my moral mission—nay, destroy my good standing as a rebel with a cause. So, I was between a rock and a hard place.

Should I plead I was criminally insane and escape the chair?

Or stay competent and get cooked like a turkey dinner?

If only I could have seen this coming all those years ago when I left my PhD program in Washington State to pursue a truer path. Then, everything had seemed so straightforward:

1. Escape the capitalist, technological society.

2. Learn to survive in nature.

3. Destroy the system from the outside with bombs. I mean, I had an honorable purpose, and wasn't just blowing people up for no good reason.

In my career, I had blown up three people and injured another twenty.

I blew up an oil executive, a genetic scientist, and a psychologist I didn't particularly like. And I didn't feel any remorse at all. These people represented the instrumental tools of the system and the society which I hated, which psychologically and spiritually broke so many!

How could I feel any remorse for them?

The system felt no guilt, plodding along, carrying all of humanity to their doom.

We had to stop the endless march of technological progress!

We had to turn back before it was too late!

"What are the odds of the chair... If I don't plead insanity?"

The little weaselly assistant looked up from his notes.

"Almost certain. You've pissed off quite a few people, Mr. Dwarkiecz. Clearly, you haven't been in control of yourself."

"I couldn't have been more in control of myself! No human being has ever been more in control of themselves than I have! This whole thing is a setup, and the head honchos are rooting for me to get barbecued, so I'll rescind my ideas and avoid becoming a martyr for the cause!"

I mean, I figured at some point, I would have to die for my ideals, as what else was there?

Life in the woods, peeing in buckets, reading obscure French Communism.

All that was training for this showdown with the system, so that I could show what monsters they really were, to become a martyr.

God, my blood boiled at the thought of the system.

I had been born into a normal family so typical of this monstrous enterprise. A mother, a father, a brother—the nuclear family if I'd ever seen one. But I was too smart, and they never understood me. I was left alone with my brain, and they had all these human relationships.

I was tested at Harvard and shown to have an IQ of 167, near-genius level.

I knew then that I had to do something special. I mean, having an IQ of that size was like being given a spaceship, or a super high-powered ray gun?

What good was it in an office clerk job that was 9-5? No, there was only one path for an intellect like mine; I had to remake the entire system. But the whole thing was fucked. Like a great pile of wriggling worms, the only chance was complete annihilation, to tear it down and start again, returning to zero with myself as the architect of the new world order.

At first, making the bombs was difficult. I couldn't even generate more than a few sparks, like your average garden firework. Bomb-making was my craft. In the beginning, I was an apprentice, making rudimentary nail bombs and Molotov cocktails. The urge to test them on a human being was growing. That was something I was asked frequently these days: how did I see other human beings? Did I see them at all, or were they just non-entities to me?

And what about their families? A lot of bloated sacks.

Who cared about one person and their insignificant life compared to the millions that would be lost if the system were allowed to continue?

We are all so settled into our roles that we can't even see we are phonies! We are phonies who perpetuate death. In war, you have to make sacrifices, and what do I care if no-one is on my side? No-one was ever on my side, so this is nothing new.

"Look, Ted," the female lawyer said, "they are going to throw the book at you. There's no way they'll let you get away with this, as you terrorised the entire country, the manhunt for you cost over 100 million dollars, you were the FBI's most wanted man, and this is a death penalty state. So, as your lawyer, the only way out of this is to plead *insanity*."

"But I'm not crazy!"

"You lived in the woods, drinking your pee, and making bombs?" the male lawyer said.

"Yes that's what I had to do for the mission! But if I plead insanity, then what about my writings? My manifesto? They become the writings of a madman?"

"It's not much better now," the pencil-pushing assistant said.

"Excuse me!"

If I hadn't been handcuffed to the table, I would have throttled him. He raised his glasses to the bridge of his nose.

"I read your manifesto, and while you seem to have a good handle on the problem, it's quite clear your solution of living in the woods and blowing people up is absurd..."

"And what do you suggest?"

He shrugged a little, and the female lawyer was looking at him with a curious air. For the first time, I could see the fluorescent office lights shining on golden earrings like a little sun.

"I mean, I was a bit of an anarchist when I was younger, then I grew up. You don't seriously believe the current state of affairs is worse than the complete annihilation of the world?"

"Yes I do, in every single way. Human beings are demoted to cogs in a machine, dehumanised, wage slaves, their lives a living horror until they go mad!"

"Still better than being dead."

The weaselly pencil-pusher shrugged. "You will be soon."

"Distractions from the rich pilfering the honeypot of globalisation, and building towards a global genocide!"

"But we have free speech. You probably could just have published your manifesto, and people could have decided, but instead, you threatened to bomb the White House if they didn't run it? I mean, how insecure can you get?"

"I made my point..." I said quietly, feeling mocked and humiliated, "I dominated the entire country, and people were terrified and feared me."

"They feared your bombs," the female lawyer interjected. "You kind of look like a meth head, and I feel sorry for you more than anything. I think if you'd had a girlfriend and a couple of friends, you'd never have thought twice about the *system*..."

"The system matters!" I shouted like a wild animal. "You are blind! Blinded! You are part of the machine and thus cannot see out, and I'll never rescind my words! Even if they do kill me! I want new lawyers, one who will understand my anti-technological views!"

My prison cell was ten feet by twelve feet, a rusty bed on a squeaky frame with a steel toilet in the corner, and that was it. It was still bigger than my own cabin, where I'd launched my counter-attack on the system. The only joy of the cabin was the butterflies that lived in the meadow outside. Watching them playing, forgetting the wilderness was always my greatest fear, losing my connection with Mother Nature. This prison cell was a cage, but the real cage was society, morality, and other people. There was no doubt in my mind that I would be put into a cage because I was born in one, one from which only destroying the world could free me. I lived every single second of my life avoiding that inevitable reality. My only regret was that I couldn't kill more, that I couldn't tear down the entire thing with a click of my fingers. There was a knock on the door, and the food flap which delivered my daily meals opened.

"Mr. Dwarkiecz, your request for a new legal team has been denied."

The flap shut again.

"Fuck you!" I shouted, "Fuck you and your legal team! You are pawns! Pawns!"

I snatched up the book I was reading from the floor, though I had no appetite for reading. It was 'Lolita' by Vladimir Nabokov. Even I, a demon of hell, found the book controversial.

A story of a paedophile and his love affair with a young teenage girl.

How could he write such a thing? Understand a monster?

By most standards, *I* was a monster, a thing in the night that frightened people. I loved that, and that was what I lived for most. The fear was intoxicating, and were I to admit I was a madman, I would be reduced to nothing more than a patient. I was screwed now, as this legal team would sink me and my credibility would go down the toilet. I could refuse? Request the death penalty? I sat back on the rusty bed and bounced on the springs. Surely, death couldn't be that bad? They'd dip the sponges in the water, and I'd watch the audience, watching me, and maybe scream some profanity—then *ahhhhh* and nothing. Freedom? I wondered, was this how Jesus Christ felt when he was about to die for his cause? God was on his side.

But I had never believed in God. Were there Atheist martyrs?

God was a fiction made for people too weak to see the truth. We were alone.

Through the window, I could see the pale moon in the night sky. The shadows of the bars fell across my cell like the stripes of a zebra. There was no escape.

I held the back of my hand in the shade and opened my palm into the moonlight. My greatest fear was forgetting the mountains and the woods, the smell of the damp mud, and wind on my face. In the woods, you didn't care if you died; you were just happy at the time to be alive, and didn't have to think too much about the future. Now, the future was in my hands?

In my throat? I supposed at a young age, I had given up on the future.

They say serial killers are the products of bad families and some sort of gene. My family was normal. Perhaps that was the cardinal sin, being so, so normal that an aberration, a stone in the shoe like me, was going to come along. I knew I was rotten fruit from birth, and that this was why everyone looked at me strangely, averted their eyes from mine, faked their laughs.

Everywhere in the world, I sought love and found only cold shoulders, turned backs. The only gift I had received was my intelligence, which only brought me to the vision of the world's end. My intelligence made me special, unique, and yet I felt more inferior than worms in the soil. Even a worm in the soil was more dignified, blind in the dirt, struggling for life.

Even that spineless invertebrate had more strength than I did.

I removed the cords from my shoe laces and fashioned them into a noose.

I pushed the bed up against the wall and tied the cord around the end of one of the legs. Then I placed the loop of the noose around my neck and lay down so the cord was taut and I felt the blood leave my head. This was it. And then the rope broke.

△▽△

I rubbed my neck as I sat at the defence table; my neck now had a big circular burn around it, as though I had choked on a halo. Everyone knew I had tried to kill myself, which would not help my plea of sanity. So, I had made up my mind in the night. My lawyer and her pencil-pushing assistant, whom I would love to throttle, were waiting for my verdict.

"So, have you decided?" she asked. "We don't have to proceed with a defence if you plead insanity."

"No..." I said definitely.

"Mr. Dwarkiecz..." the judge asked, and I stood up. I stood up in front of the jury, the audience, the television cameras. I was prepared to tell them all about the system, about the technological, industrial society's collapse, the rise of the robots, and the eventual end of humanity, the whole story, not a moment of detail spared.

"You stand trial on ten counts of illegally transporting, mailing, and using bombs, and three counts of murder. How do you plead?" I felt the handcuffs on my hands, the handcuffs on my feet, the cord around my neck last night, and the shadows of the bars on my open palm.

"Guilty," I told him. "Guilty on all charges."

The Forgotten One

North Dublin, June 2064

IT WAS THE START of a summer of violence.

On the lower half, the streetlights were older, rusted, unmaintained, and underneath one of them stood my contact, Jimmy McSean, a double agent who didn't look bright enough to be an agent at all. He was staring up at the streetlights, a dim look on his face, the wrinkled bags sagging beneath his slitty eyes and fluffy pubescent beard.

"Don't you love the old street lights over this side?" he said. "I think they're just marvellous."

"They don't work..." I said, watching the lamp light flickering.

"That gives them their character..." Jimmy said, glancing around suspiciously. We didn't have time to waste on idle chit chat, however, as there was a mission. The lower half lived in filth and dirt, like pigs, and it was notoriously dangerous, so they didn't want to hang around too long. I was from the upper half, which used to be the Southside of Dublin, fifty years ago.

Dublin was a prosperous place and for a long time, the whole country benefitted, until the invention of self-driving cars. A huge proportion of men became unemployed, hopeless, and turned against the rest, succeeding from the wealthier upper half and taking up residence in North Dublin, which became known as the lower half. The world of 2064 was a very different place from the millenium. Not so hopeful, tense, and filled with warfare.

"Is the meeting nearby?"

Jimmy nodded.

"In the docklands..."

The streets were quiet and abandoned. No-one had jobs or moved around at night, so I was surprised when we turned a corner to where the meeting was taking place and ran into a group of ragged men. They were huddled close together in conversation and I could smell the sweat from their bodies. They had dirt on their clothes, scars and wounds on their faces, and their eyes opened wide and looked startled like prey animals as we approached.

Even though my disguise was elaborate, complete with scars, bruises and lacerations of my own, there were some things you couldn't just fake, such as actually knowing people, and being known. I was looking to Jimmy to make the introductions but he just hovered around, stupidly staring at the streetlights. I would be killed if I were to get found out, for certain.

"Who are you?" a man asked at the front of the warehouse entrance, and the group turned to face and block my way. Above their shoulders, I could see that the inside of the warehouse was lit. Our intelligence said *he* would be here tonight. I nudged Jimmy, who did nothing.

"Twine," I said just as I'd rehearsed. "Jake Twine, just out of prison, and I'm here for the meeting..."

I was as bold as I could be with a lyrical Dublin accent, and had been chosen for this mission because I was the best actress the upper half had to offer, even better than most of the men.

"I've never seen you before." He pouted his upper lip like a proud primate, believing he had outsmarted me.

"Howiye, Pat," Jimmy said, still looking at the streetlights, "Jake's with me..."

"I wasn't talkin' to you, Jimmy! I don't like the look of this chap."

He stepped forward, drawing himself up to his full height, staring down; show time. I pulled my shoulders back and puffed up my chest.

"What I don't like is that we live in a technological hellhole! That everything we do is monitored, checked and catalogued, and that we are human farm animals for powerful and shady people!" He seemed taken aback. "Now get out of my way so I can put a stop to it!"

There was a murmur through the men who stepped out of the way, and even Jimmy seemed surprised and had looked away from the streetlights for the first time.

"Alright then," I said and fixed my coat. "Lead the way, Jimmy!"

In my whole life, I'd never known anything but the upper half. The Supreme Leader was like a father to me; he had taken me in when my parents were killed in a lower-half explosion.

He saw my potential, my determination, and nurtured the fire within me. I was top of my class through school and university, a classically trained actress as well as a security agent and attended one of the best educated places in the modern world.

There was not a qualification or award or honor that I did not have, except for the mask of the Forgotten One hanging on my mantelpiece, and that was coming. Inside the room was grubby and smelt of leaked sewage, so maybe this was an old treatment plant.

The men were gathered in the center of the room and lit by candle light, since electricity was now even too far for these zealots. Electricity was a tool of the modern world, a world they hated and had rejected down to the microscopic level. I strode forward purposefully, confident in my disguise and my abilities, and many moved out of the way for me.

"Look, you know what I mean," a man said in a thick Irish accent. "You take the bomb, leave it under the drain and when the cars drive on, *boom*. Capiche?"

"Capiche?"

The man took a hold of his shoulders and shook him.

"D'ya understand what I'm saying?"

"Oh, yeah. Ok so, just over at..."

The man in charge struck him on the face, he fell silent.

"That's enough talk. You know well where to go."

The smaller, subservient man dispersed, taking a small, brown box, like a cask of wine and leaving the way I had come in.

I tried to see which way he was going. To deliver another bomb, no doubt, but to whom?

"Over here," Jimmy said, "over here..."

He directed me to a stool not far away from a foul-smelling sewer drain, and I supposed this was as good a place to die as any. From the back of the room, there was a heavy knocking.

The man scurried over and Jimmy nodded his head. It was the Forgotten One. He stepped out of the storm drain and was about six-and-a-half feet tall, with heaps of fur rugs on him like a cloak. Yet, the most disturbing thing about him was the mask he wore, made of iron, like a Roman dramatic mask pulled downward into a permanent frown.

He was a fearful sight and a cold shiver ran up my spine.

I felt the grip of a gun hidden beneath the breastplate.

I wasn't supposed to kill him but my intellect told me not to waste this opportunity, that it might not come around again. I was to radio the squad nearby and have the place surrounded, but I knew well by then he would be gone, back into the endless maze of old sewer ducts in which we could never find him. He had evaded us since the split in 2040, when I was just a child. But now, I was an adult and he wouldn't get away so easily.

He strode about with the air of a university lecturer in front of his students. Like a professor, he waved his arms in the air.

"We stand on this, the eve of our deliverance..."

He threw his fist in the air, and the men cheered.

"A long time ago, before any of you remember, even before the millennium, there was a man called Ted Dwarkiecz, a freedom fighter like us. He saw the danger the technology posed and he died a hero, a martyr to try and stop the senseless progress! This world had become too complex for its inhabitants, too deceitful, too rational, and too intelligent.

"What chance did any of us have? We had no-one to be anymore, so we became criminals, thugs, outcasts, but now we can be freedom fighters, heralds of a new world!

"We may have to lay down our lives like Ted Dwarkiecz did, but we will join him in the line of fighters against the technological world! As heroes!

"By this time tomorrow evening, the Supreme Leader will be dead, and once again peace and opportunity will be for everyone, not just the few, but for the many."

I removed the gun from my breastplate, holding it close at my side.

"Did you ever feel anyone gave a damn if you lived or died?" the Forgotten One said to the man closest to him.

"Just you, sir..."

He strode theatrically in a circle.

"Did you ever feel this society cared about you?" he said to Jimmy who averted his wrinkled bag eyes from the iron mask, which then turned to me.

"And what about you? Did you ever feel your society loved you?"

I removed the gun from my waist and placed it at point-blank range to his chest.

"Honestly, I don't care," I said and pulled the trigger, seeing how the blast blew him backwards. It deafened me. I fired again and again but to my surprise, he was wriggling away, towards the storm drain. I shot at the Forgotten One close enough to kill him, so was he wearing armour? No primitive body armour would stop a caliber of this size.

He fell back to the trap door as I kept firing, each bullet missing like the last until the trigger clicked. His mask was loose and underneath, I caught sight of his face. It was a terribly plain face, the face of nobody, and then they caught up with me. The first punch came down on my cheek from the side, the next the back, then I was swarmed. I'd never been beaten before, never experienced that sensation of losing all control. The crowd dived on me like a swarm of locusts, kicking, punching, biting, until the world faded to black.

△▽△

The Supreme Leader is not going to be happy with this, was my first thought as I woke up in Tallaght Hospital. Two black eyes, broken nose, broken ribs, missing teeth, twisted ankle.

But none of the wounds hurt as much as the fact that I had clearly been outfoxed. Why was he wearing armour? That kind of armour was a recent invention. Modern? What was really going on? I tried to sit up in bed, feeling the bruising of my kidneys and back. It seemed whatever way I turned, I was discovering new symphonies of pain. Life was going to be very difficult, and stopping whatever was going to happen tonight was nigh impossible at this rate.

"I can feel that," the Supreme said.

He was a squat man with a slight bulge in his head from the neuralink implant. He was a sympoit, a human who had fused with the AI system which controlled the city.

"Supreme Leader," I said and stood up, coughing and sitting back down in a hurry.

He was kind of like a dad who had never had any kids, and at times, it was hard to know where I stood with him.

"Sit down, sit down, don't hurt yourself." He wore an open purple shirt with dark slacks, and carried a white dog beneath his arm. His eyes were exceptionally blue like lightning, and juxtaposed to the snowy whiteness of his hair. He was the wealthiest, most powerful man in the country but for the most part, looked just like everyone else.

"I'm ok, Sir, ready to get back on duty."

"That won't be necessary, Mrs. Sharpe," he said. I could tell he was reading my vitals, I felt the morphine seep into my veins and he inclined his head.

"A little something to take the edge off. Who said I couldn't be fun? So... You tried to kill him? I forgot that was that part of the mission, that you were an assassin now? Where did you get the gun?"

I felt slightly vulnerable. His ability to interface with any technology was a superpower when you were hooked up to an IV. He could kill me if he wanted, and it seemed I could trust no-one now. "I stole it from the armoury. I wanted to settle things. You don't understand how dangerous these people are, and we can't let them live anymore."

The Supreme Leader inclined his eyebrows.

"We can't kill them either. Just because you don't get along with someone doesn't mean that you can kill them, Mrs. Sharpe. I have learned that. Maybe you were too young and inexperienced for this duty."

"They have a plan to kill you tomorrow evening? Is that harmless?"

He slammed his fist down on the bedside table and rattled the IV.

"You've become obsessed with this, Veronica. We aren't at war. We have a group of people who aren't happy with our technological advances, yet have benefitted from them..."

"It has created them! You don't understand..."

"I understand that you are consumed by thoughts of revenge for a personal vendetta and we can't use you anymore, Veronica." I didn't know what else to say.

"They have a plan, a plan tonight to take you out. To kill you!" He shook his head.

"We aren't fighting that kind of war."

"We shouldn't underestimate them!"

"Yes, you did that and we saw how well that went for you. You are lucky to be alive, and I am surprised that they did not kill you when they had the chance."

My face turned red with shame and he adjusted his collar.

"Tonight is the anniversary of the legalisation of the autonomous vehicle, and there's going to be a presentation at the customs house."

"Over the river?"

"Yes. Security has everything under control." He seemed so certain. All that information had gone to his head, and he was walking right into a trap.

"Please," I said, "They have a plan! It's not safe! Shut it down"

"This is not a tyranny...You're off the job, Veronica. It was a mistake to begin with, getting you involved." Suddenly, I had an idea.

"I saw his face. Can I review the data vault? Maybe I can ID him?"

He thought for a moment before sighing.

"Fine, if it'll make you feel better." He motioned to the two green-uniformed soldiers with their assault rifles. They were escorting him.

"Get Mrs. Sharpe discharged and take her to the data vault."

He looked me up and down like a worn-out teacher.

"And then take her home!"

I was marched down the fluorescent lit corridors, unsure if I was a prisoner or still an employee. The two sentries stood close behind and each was armed; was I being frog-marched?

The data vault was the operations intelligence control room for the upper half, essentially the home to a supercomputer that kept data on every civilian in the city.

For years since the construction of the internet, this supercomputer had been sorting out each individual citizen's digital footprint and building a profile. The nerve center held every text message, every photograph, every Facebook post, comment and like a person had ever made, and you could walk through their life via the data vault simulation.

I stood at the door of there and entered in my code—which was rejected. The keypad flashed red. So, I had been blacklisted.

"Updates," the sentry said and flashed his own badge which went green immediately.

I knew there were no updates, and that my impulsive actions had made me into an enemy of the state, just like the rebels. We entered the control room which was a portal door with a space suit in the middle. Not literally a spacesuit, but more like an MRI machine in which you were lowered into a virtual display. "Step into the machine please," one of the sentries said.

I was hesitant. If they were going to take me out, this was the perfect place and time to do it. Incapacitated, I'd never even wake up. Was this a set-up? What choice did I have?

If I backed out now, they would be more suspicious. I had never entered the machine before, although previously, I had guided other people through the procedure, so knew what I was doing, at least from the outside.

"Do you understand the procedure?"

"No," I said, playing dumb. "I will need you to guide me through it."

The men understood and I was put under.

The most unnerving thing about the simulation machine was that you acquired 360-degree vision. A larger visual field allowed for more stimuli, so you became a sort of brain made of eyes. They would walk me through the lives of some people they suspected first, and then I would be exposed to the entire civilian populace.

The process started like a video game, and then quickly, I was plunged into the data world. You couldn't navigate this data by conscious thought, which was why the technician was there to steer, but I didn't know that certain individuals by instinct alone could shape the journey. Ever so slightly, I started to influence the indigestible sea of information.

"Do you recognise this person? What about this one? Did he speak like this? Look like this? Does this fit the profile?" I was playing a dual game, keeping the sentries satisfied but also at the same time searching for who the Forgotten One really was.

I was in the addresses of old defectors, and there was something I recognised: an apartment. And I steered through there.

"Do you see something?"

"He might have mentioned this address? Do we have photographs?"

Suddenly in the first person, I was in the apartment, walking around.

The darkened wood was familiar, though none of the furniture looked the same. Weak light filtered through the grey, veil-like, curtains frozen in time, and the house looked abandoned. Down the hall I headed, to where I knew there was a bedroom on the right.

"What is this place?" the sentries asked. "Is this where he lived?"

"Ehh, I don't know. I've never been here," I lied. I turned the corner and sure enough, there was a wardrobe, large and antique, a greenish wood with round knob handles.

"Who lived in this accommodation?" I asked.

"A Mr. Charles Freely." Suddenly, an image flashed up of a man with red hair, blue eyes and a scowling, tough-looking face; he was about six-and-a-half feet tall.

"Is this the man we are looking for?"

"Who is he?" I reply.

"That is classified, I am afraid."

"No," I said. "That's not him. Now take me over to the other side. I want to see the lower half in more detail…"

I was sent home in a car to my flat near D'olier Street, a top floor apartment, right facing the other side. The gates, the hordes of people on the other side… Strange how these technologies did nothing to bring us together but only seemed to force us further apart. That was the cost of progress, the Supreme Leader said. And I liked to be close to the other side.

It gave me a sense of the possibility of completing my mission. I did remember the man, as he had been there the day my parents were taken. Was he the one who killed them? I spent the hours afterwards hiding in my closet, too scared to leave. Ever since that day, I'd suffered a dreadful claustrophobia. My father was an upstanding businessman of repute, and my mother, a lawyer, sat on the city council. He robbed me of that perfect childhood, and instead, I had this lonely uphill, painful journey. He would pay for that.

The pain in my body wasn't life-threatening but it was certainly getting there, and only my mind was willing to go on. The car stopped in a convoy of vehicles along the queues waiting to pass through the gates on the bridges. They would be going left and I would be going right. I pressed on the GPS of the vehicle. The Supreme Leader crackled on the intercom, "Looking for a detour, Mrs. Sharpe?"

"Eh, the air conditioning… I'm roasted."

"Sudden fever?"

"I just need some air."

He switched on the air conditioning,

"You know, maybe I need some proper air. Let me out a few streets early and I'll walk."

"Veronica," he said. "I know what you are like. Do you really think I'm falling for that?"

"So, I am a prisoner?"

"No, you can leave if you want."

"The door is locked."

"I worry about you," he said.

"You should be worrying about yourself."

There was no reply on the intercom.

"You know I always loved you like a daughter..."

"I didn't know that."

"I know I can be cold, impersonal but I value your safety, I care" said the Supreme Leader.

"Can we speak about this later?" I said. There wasn't time.

The Supreme Leader cleared his throat.

"Yes, of course."

He unlocked the car and I pushed open the door to the cool air of the quays.

"Thank you," I said. "Max..." That was his real name, and not one I had ever said before.

"You are welcome, Veronica, take care of yourself..." he said, and he was still talking but I'd already closed the door. The walk along the Quays was cold and refreshing, and some refugees from the other side had gathered around.

Strange how now he wanted to play Dad? Stranger still that I'd spent my whole life seeking his approval—the academy, the training, everything. And when I was finally finished, then what? So typical. I had no time for men anymore. Not for fathers, husbands, boyfriends...

I just wanted my revenge for the death of my parents, and that was that.

Across the black water of the Liffey was the lower half where I had to be, but swimming was cold, unfriendly, and possibly hazardous in my current condition.

I could try and blag my way through the gates, though no doubt they would be on high alert. That was when I spied a familiar face of someone walking around the upper half like a lost man. "Jimmy!" I said and nearly hugged him, so happy to see him. He was as surprised as I was, his wrinkled, up-opened eyes squinting at me.

"Oh," he said, "I thought you were dead..."

"Nearly was. What happened to you?"

"I, eh, left, for good," he said and sniffled a little bit. "I can't go back anymore. How am I going to save the streetlights now?" Goddammit, not the streetlights again!

"The streetlights don't matter, Jimmy. There's bigger fish to fry!" He stared up at the high lamppost on the Southern side, high, angular, modern things like out of Star Trek.

"But I like the old ones."

"These ones use no electricity. They are great for the environment."

Jimmy shook his head. "But who could love them?"

I shook my head. *Only you could love streetlights, Jimmy,* I thought in my head.

"I need you to take me to the Forgotten One. I need to stop him before he kills the Supreme Leader tonight." Jimmy shook his head,

"I don't care. Why would I?"

"If we save him, I could ask about the streetlights. He could save them."

Jimmy looked excited and then his brow furrowed, and he pulled me down to the pavement as nearby, a massive explosion ripped through the night. The size of a one-ton bomb, cars, people, and chunks of gate were thrown into the Liffey as O'Connell Bridge was no more. The street lights faded and went out. The Supreme Leader!

Had they killed the Supreme Leader? Jimmy pulled a screwdriver from his bag pocket.

"Follow me," he said. I hesitated at the mouth of the pipe, terrified of tight spaces, but I could hear gunshot and volleys from the other side, cheers, and clashes.

"Come on!" Jimmy said, "we don't have time!"

I climbed into the drain behind him.

The tunnel was like a tomb; you couldn't see anything, and down there, the air smelt like rancid silage. My feet splashed in the water, and I imagined rats and spiders and big giant cobwebs, feeling the weight of the Liffey water pressing down above us.

I thought the anxiety was going to overwhelm me, but Jimmy led the way, his wrinkled eyes better adapted to the darkness.

No wonder he liked the street lights, as they were heaven compared to down here. After what seemed like forever of crawling, we reached the end of the pipe.

"Where are we going?"

We pushed forward and forward until we came to a grate and popped it out of the wall.

The room was filled with casks of wine in dusty round kegs and there was no-one else there. Jimmy motioned to get out.

He pointed upwards, and I could hear boots and heavy marching through the stone.

"Base," he said, opening his eyes so I knew what he meant.

"Thank you, Jimmy," I said and kissed his cheek, "I'll stick to my word and do what I can for the streetlights." He nodded and leapt back into the sewer.

I faced the stone staircase, to go and face my fate.

Thanks to all the mud, swelling and general decay, I actually looked like someone from the lower half, and was probably even better disguised than I'd been the last time. This time, the bruises were real, the scars were real, and the wounds were open.

"We've blown the bridge!" a messenger shouted, and there were whoops and cheers, and the forgotten one sat there stoically, not even wearing his mask.

He was pale and unwell-looking, not taking part in the action.

"They've confirmed that the Supreme Leader is dead. The neural-ink is down and the city is ours!"

Charles McFreely. He looked like anybody, any man who'd had a hard paper round in life. I lifted a gun from nearby propped up against a barrel, and pointed it at his head, no more than a few feet away. His eyes widened and narrowed but his posture did not change.

"You again..." he said. "What more do you want? The Supreme Leader is dead."

"Revenge," I said. "Same as before."

"For that bastard?"

"No, for my parents..."

"I never knew your parents. Do you not see where we are? This is no place for revenge..." I looked around, seeing we were in an old disused church, not too far from the altar.

The pews were scattered in all directions, and above, the pillars stretched for miles, holding up what was left of the roof.

"This is the only church left," he said, "on the upper or lower side. All the others were destroyed when your Supreme Leader took his power, left to ruin..."

"Who are you and why did you kill my parents?"

"I'm not sure I did, to be fair. Who're your parents?"

"Why were you in 17, Barnely Way all those years ago? Before it was blown up by you?" He stopped and all the blood drained from his red face till there was nothing left. He was almost as transparent as the Supreme Leader when he collected himself.

"I haven't heard that name in a long time—twenty-four years to be precise."

"Well I was born there, and my parents lived in that house before you killed them…"

"Funny," he said and fixed his dark eyes on me. They were red-tinged and murky, painted with blood.

"I lived there, lived there for twenty years since I came up from Cork. Married a woman who was a lawyer and I had a daughter who'd a shock of red hair."

"What!" I burst out, cheeks burning hot with shame.

"I'm your Da," he said and smiled, weakly as he could. "Ironic isn't it…"

"You are lying."

"I was an engineer, a working man, and we built these roads, the houses, these streetlights… Then everyone forgot, tried to replace us, and pretend we never existed in the first place. I put my foot down and was a powerful enough man, well-liked, so others put their foot down with me. The Supreme Leader tried to make an example of me, your mother was killed in the explosion. I escaped and I've been seeking my revenge ever since…"

"But you're murderers. You're the bad guys."

"We'd rather die than lose our freedom. Progress took everything we had and left us with nothing. Were we supposed to be grateful? This new world isn't a utopia; it's a prison."

He started laughing and coughed, a little blood flecking on his lips.

"I won't be in it for much longer anyway…"

"What?" I said, battered by the mixture of emotions. He raised his coat to show where the bullets had gone in, several shots having penetrated the cheap flimsy homemade armour. He hadn't broken his code.

"You've had your revenge," he said. "I've not long left now."

I had never had a dad. I didn't know how to feel about the man in front of me. He was no more my father than the rain falling on a muddy puddle. The Supreme Leader was more a father than he was, and he was dead. He was responsible for my parents' death?

"Just because you don't get along with someone doesn't mean that you can kill them, Mrs. Sharpe. I have learned that." No.

For the first time, I noticed the frightened and scowling men around the edges of our conversation, hundreds of them, invisible, unseen, unheard, left behind in the darkness and shadows. They would kill me this time.

"You're lying" I decided, "it's just a story, you were angry, so you made it up..."

"Finish me off, then..." he said. "It's your right."

I held the gun, the cold weight, and looked beyond the man, to the chips of the stained-glass window, a nail through a hand, a world composed of smoke, dust, and the weak streetlights which came alive in the hot summer night; blinking.

Launderette for Losers

I HURRIED ACROSS THE rain-crossed street of Warschauer Straße, Berlin. Through my plastic bag, the yellow dress shone out like a reminder of how much of an idiot I was. I thought Julie would like the dress, and by extension, would like me. Julie was twenty years old, slim and attractive, a naked magazine model and cat fanatic. She was a lot like a cat too, did what she wanted when she wanted, while I was more of a dog person really.

My heels slipped on the curb as I stepped from the road and onto the pavement. I had followed her to *The Basement Bar* against my better judgement, as my desire was to go somewhere high society, somewhere with a rooftop view and fireworks. Instead, we ended up underground and soaked in Jameson and ginger ale. When would I learn my lesson?

I stepped into the glow of the brightly lit 115 Waschsalon. Through the three front windows, the chrome faces of the machines glinted in the fluorescent office lights.

Who even used launderettes anymore?

They seemed a half deviant place, somewhere between a sex club and a dentist's office. One of those places devoid of humans, like an abandoned mineshaft. I just knew I had to get the stain off this dress so I could forget about this evening. Truth was, I didn't even like the dress. It was like something I had worn when I was sixteen, when I had been trying too hard.

I opened the glass door, the steady hum of the washing machines enveloping my ears.

It was like being inside a stationary spaceship, threatening to take off at every minute.

I thought I was alone, but a deep phlegmy cough came from the other side of the room and drew my attention. It was the kind of cough one could only acquire by trying to smoke their way through a chest infection. I knew the stubborn, husky rattle well.

A pale, middle-aged man sat on the row of machines by the left wall, his legs spread wide open, and a bottle of brown beer clutched between the crotch of his dark jeans. He had slicked-back hair, a face like an old boxing bag, and a green crucifix tattooed on each of his middle fingers, the wrong way around, like the antichrist. He sniffed his nose at me and combed back his hair as though the breeze I'd let in from the door had dislodged his fringe. He seemed incredibly familiar, but so did every other dickhead in the world; I knew the type.

I worked in customer service and dealt with middle-aged men who believed the world revolved around them every day, men who put up fights in the most absurd of situations, and seemed to resort to anything short of murder to be proven right.

My boots squeaked on the floor as I turned my back to him and started to study the German instructions printed on the wall above the machines. I didn't know German. Life was too short to learn it, and my own had been frantic enough of late. From the pictures on the walls and some common sense, I figured the machines were coin-operated. I removed a few shiny wet euros from my black jacket pocket because that was what the machine ate, and one by one, slotted my sacrifices inside. The coins made no sound, and I had the impression they were falling off the edge of a cliff and into a deep and bottomless gorge.

Nothing happened.

"Fuck," I said under my breath.

"Drücken Sie den grünen Knopf..." the pale man called from the other side of the room. Drücken meant to print, which wasn't particularly useful. Print what?

"Eh-súl-I-gun?" I said.

"Oh... you're English," he said with a posh British accent.

"Hit the button!" he said. "The green one!" And I pushed.

"I said *hit* it!" He had that kind of harsh English accent that was so off-putting I could barely muster the willpower to follow his direction, but sure enough, I hit the button as if my life depended on it and the water started pumping in. A wave of relief rolled over me.

"Thanks," I said, "I really need to get this cleaned..."

He shrugged.

"Brute force and ignorance, mate."

"Weird place, isn't it? Like, who doesn't have washing machines anymore?"

"Lots," he said and went back to his beer.

"Can I have one?"

He laughed in a deep, guttural way, and I thought he was going to start coughing again. His teeth were short and sharp like a shark's, and his two eyebrows pulled into a mono-brow, united by a tuft of goat-like hair which was fearful and primitive.

"Are you Irish?"

"Yes..." This news seemed to warm him up.

"My gran's from Ir-land. My last name's Green."

Was Green an Irish surname? Surely, if any name was, it was one bearing our national colour.

"Eric..." he said, and handed over a bottle, "Eric Green."

"I'm Diana," I told him, "like the princess…"

In Berlin, it was legal to drink anywhere. Seeing people on the street drinking was familiar, but you never saw anyone drunk like in Ireland. Eric looked as though he got very drunk, like a washed-up actor, vengeful drunk. He didn't offer to open my bottle, and finally, I dug into the bottom of my bag and removed a lighter.

"Can I have that?" he said.

"I'm using it," I told him as I opened the beer. He had no manners. He didn't even look sorry, not one bit—not one measly percent embarrassed.

I handed over the lighter, and he lit his fag, taking in a significant drag.

"Can I have a cigarette?" I asked, feeling as though I had to be bolder in his presence than I had been lately. People usually offered me things though.

"Why?" he said.

"Eh, because they cost two euros."

"I could retire on two euros. You wouldn't ask me for two euros, wouldya?"

"I might…"

"Well, you could get stuffed, mate."

"I quit anyway…"

"When?"

"New Year's resolution."

The smoke looked utterly out of place in the launderette, like lighting up in a doctor's office, but there was no-one to tell him off. The launderette was run by an indifferent and robotic God.

"So you've been clear a whole twenty-four hours then. Congratulations."

He played with the lighter, spinning it around and around in circles. His legs were short and dangled in front of the machine lid, and he kicked the door loudly.

"Can you not do that?" I said, getting annoyed.

"What made you quit?' he said, as if cancer, death, and breathlessness weren't reason enough, as if there must be something else, something more wrong.

"I just felt something had to change. I wanted to be different…"

Eric blew smoke from the side of his mouth, like a tea kettle.

"Everybody wants change, change, change, but nobody wants to do a damn thing to get it. I wanted a change and I walked to Sweden. You ever walked to Sweden? Now there's a change. I smoked the whole way too, not a penny to my name, didn't ask nothing from no-one. Ate berries and shit in bushes. Best time of my whole life, I'd do it again tomorrow if I could."

"You've a unique perspective; I'll give you that."

I was terrible at arguing against people. It seemed that as soon as they finished their point, all I could do was nod my head and agree. But I didn't agree with a word he was saying. As if walking to Sweden and quitting smoking were the same thing. Not one bit.

"Did someone break your 'art?" He eyed me up, saying, "you look a bit peaky."

I thought this was genuine sympathy.

"Well, yes, actually," I said.

"You're a dike, aren't ye?"

"Ah, for fuck…"

"I'd know a dike anywhere except Holland!"

He laughed loudly, and I got nervous. Everything he did made me nervous that he was going to spill or break something or just outright cause a scene. I was glad we were the only two there. I wanted to change the topic.

"How do you think this place stays in business?" I said. "Surely everyone has washing machines now."

He shrugged.

"You don't..."

"I do! Mine broke. Surely, not enough people are breaking washing machines every day to keep this place in business. Either way, it's a conspiracy..." When the washing machine had broken at home, Julie just stood there putting on lip gloss while I ran around, grabbing towels, plugging drains, moving furniture, all while on the phone to the repair person.

"Can you help?" I pleaded.

"Looks like you've got it under control," she said and returned to her lip gloss.

"*I* never had a washing machine," he said, "I don't even have a toilet...Well, sort of..."

"How do you sort of have a toilet?"

"We have a place we go, but that doesn't make it a toilet, does it?"

I took a sip of the beer. It was sour but pleasant.

"I'm off the grid," he said, "don't have a washing machine, a phone, a toilet, nothing. I'm a free man."

"How do you live without a washing machine?"

"Just fine," He said and picked his nose, "I have a system..."

"A system?"

He turned so he could elaborate further. "I've got seven pairs of clothes in a chest of drawers. I wear one pair of clothes a day and put the others in the drawer until they are clean again..."

"Wait, what do you mean, clean again?"

He raised his hands to God.

"It's like magic, mate...You take them out, good as new!"

I shook my head in disbelief.

"I'm surprised you don't smell."

He glanced over his shoulder as he stubbed out his cigarette.

"You normal people aren't living. It's all, *ohh, I better say sorry and wash my clothes*. You're sheep, the lot of you. I'm living."

"What do you do?" I asked him.

"A little bit of everything. Everything you don't do, that's me."

Suddenly it dawned on me; I did know him. I remembered seeing him through the packed dance-floor, through the crowds. He was in a dark shirt, serving drinks behind the bar, and he gave Julie a Jameson and ginger ale instead of the two shots of Jäger she ordered, and when they argued for a refund, he just flat out refused. I said it was fine and tried to bring the drink back to our table and then, uh oh. I hoped he didn't remember what happened next. I uncrossed my legs and rubbed my tights nervously.

"I work in the Basement Bar. I do what I want though, so if I don't want to serve someone, I'll tell them to fuck off."

"That's nice. I work in customer service, so we have to deal with everyone..."

"Ohh, I love customer service departments."

"Really?"

"I love arguing with them! I've been locked in this battle with the post office for seven months. One day, I'm going to go in and shoot all those bastards!" He said this with such glee, it was as if he was going to a picnic.

"I was actually in the Basement," I said "for New Year's..."

"Oh yeah, I remember you."

"What? How do you remember me?"

"Cause you were wearing that godawful yellow dress, and you looked like a bloody banana!"

"Hey, fuck you! I like that dress, and it's not my fault your bar is full of crummy degenerates who don't wash their clothes and look like they're homeless..."

He laughed.

"I think you were the first person to ever wear yellow in that bar."

"Kandinsky says some people find yellow unsettling..."

"Kandinsky's a wanker...You were with someone, weren't you?"

"A friend..."

"A girl?"

"A girlfriend?" he teased.

"I thought she might be, but I was wrong..."

Seeing her beneath the fireworks of Frankfurter Allee and seeing the fireworks reflect on her green eyes, I thought she must be the one. Maybe she still was? Part of me knew that wasn't true; another part needed the fantasy to survive.

"She was a proper tasty piece of gear, mate, right naughty!" He shook my hand.

"Yes, she was..."

"Oh, what happened? She break your 'art?"

"She organised a threesome with this bloke..." Eric nearly spat out his beer.

"She did what? The cheeky cow..."

"I went to the bathroom to clean off the beer and she had some big blonde surfer guy. Yeah, she wanted us to get it on..."

Eric howled like a hyena.

"If you're looking for a fourth mate... I've my Speedos in my car. Was she not a lesbian?"

"She's just young, experimenting. It's just, I wanted something more serious, I guess a partner. Maybe if I'm patient, she'll change her mind." I watched the spark of my yellow dress turning around and around in the machine. I hoped the stain would come off, and tried to imagine it disappearing in my mind, but the ugly orange ring remained.

"Fuck that, mate. If she doesn't respect you and you let her, she never will. What age are you?"

"Twenty-four..."

"Well, I'm thirty-four, and if there's anything I've learned, it's if you don't stand up for yourself, no-one's gonna do it for you, sweetheart. I've been a sailor in the Gulf of Mexico, an oil rigger off the coast of New Zealand, a gold miner in the American Midwest, and one thing's true everywhere. You find the balls or you lose. End of."

"But that's just not nice. She has her way of doing things, and I have mine. Can't we all get along?"

"No, chalk and cheese don't have a birthday party together. Not without a bit of breast milk flying!"

One of the bigger machines stopped spinning, and the room dropped an audible octave.

Eric jumped off the machine and unclipped the latch. The wash was empty, and he lifted a big basin filled with oil and started pouring the juice into the device.

"Wait," I said, "Do you work here as well?"

He nodded and kicked one of the lower machines.

"Somebody has to keep an eye on these lot."

We didn't speak after that. Soon, my wash was finished and nervously, I unclipped the latch and removed my single item which had been buffed and dried to leave it without a stain.

My heart sank slightly. I could bring the dress back to Julie, wear it the next weekend, and have my heart broken all over again.

"You should fuckin' throw it in the bin, mate," Eric said, "Yellow's a stinking colour!"

The yellow had become a faded neon lime like a seasick iguana.

"Kandinsky might be a wanker," I said, "but he's right about one thing. There is something unsettling about yellow things..."

I balled up the dress and threw the whole thing straight in the bin.

"Thanks, Eric," I said and headed for the door.

"Thank you for what?" he said, surprised.

"For being such a prick."

The Man with a Mirror Face

Berlin, Christmas Eve.

PADDY HAD NOT WORN shoes all day. In fact, Paddy had not worn shoes all week; his feet were dirty and caked in ink. Paddy was supposed to be a writer, but he spent his time doing copious amounts of drugs and thrashing around his small room apartment instead.

The place where Paddy lived was called the Tin Elephant because it was made of tin, and during a storm, the rain on the roof sounded like a herd of tiny elephants.

Originally an office building, the Tin Elephant was used for squatting artists who survived on nothing other than beer and cigarettes. Three people had died in the place during the time Paddy had lived there. A teenage girl overdosed on heroin, an overweight party animal hung himself, and a young DJ choked to death on his own vomit.

Paddy wasn't in Ireland anymore.

It was his first time living abroad, and Christmas without his family. Paddy had one friend named Lorenzo, whom he visited between his bouts of drug-frenzied work. Lorenzo was a large, muscular Italian with his head painted yellow like a tennis ball, and he always wore a sort of Apollo 11, 1960s jumpsuit like that of an astronaut. He also had basically every drug ever invented by human beings, which was a real selling point for Paddy. Lorenzo had a soft spot for Paddy too, because Paddy had grown up so rich that he had no respect for anyone, and so would happily say things to Lorenzo, which others would not. Lorenzo was poor and had nothing, and so was always intrigued by the wealthy young Irish prince and his tragic outlook on life.

Why did the ones who had so much seem to suffer the most? He could never understand.

"Life is meaningless, Lorenzo," Paddy said, looking at his dirty, hobbit feet. "I've thought about it. I've thought about it a lot…"

He looked up at Lorenzo with his big blue Irish eyes and his curly brown hair, looking like a young Peter Pan. "The sooner we all die, the better…"

Lorenzo slapped him on the cheek.

"ESTUPIDO!" Lorenzo said, a comment which he frequently made about Paddy.

Lorenzo wanted the best for Paddy, but he was also himself a drug-addled Italian who traded blowjobs for heroin.

He didn't really have any moral foothold on the world to offer his friend.

"No more," Lorenzo said, taking away the drugs from Paddy.

"Oh, come on, Lorenzo, don't be like that."

"No, you are talking a COMPLETE SHIT-A, and I will not support this NO-SENSE. You are so ESTUPIDO!" Of course, Lorenzo thought he was estupido. Paddy felt pretty estupido, too. In school in Ireland, he had been a near world-class golfer, a promising student, and a talented writer. Here, he was probably one step away from being a fully-fledged crackhead, literally a hop and a skip away from the crematorium.

His parents, worried sick, called him so frequently he'd basically stopped answering.

He had no career, no future, and all his chickens were in the basket of becoming a famous artist, a dream which was fading more and more. He reached behind to scratch his arse, and realised he had sat on the latest attempt at writing. He had writer's block, and this was how a lot of his best work was ruined: he sat on his art.

Paddy wondered if Joyce or Hemingway suffered from the same *glutinium ab obscrutum* as he had? Did their arses have it out for them? Where did art even come from?

If he could just find that place, then he wouldn't have to torture himself and *do the work*, as they said. Paddy didn't even have what they would call a work ethic.

He relied on random chaos, chance, and fortune to poke and prod him onto the page, and his opportunities for work had been getting fewer and fewer.

"Something else then. Any GHB?"

"No, you DIE like the last time!" Suddenly, Lorenzo had an idea. He had just the thing to put him right. In fact, maybe even better than right. Of course, this made sense to Lorenzo.

The only thing that could solve a drug addiction was another drug!

He flipped open his suitcase, like a builder's toolbox, and rifled through it. But what kind of drug? Paddy came up behind him,

"Oh what about some coke? Or E's? Even a paracetamol at this point?"

Lorenzo searched around in the bag and pulled from his case a little vial filled with black flakes that looked like powdered volcano dust. Taking out the vial, he popped the top, and the smell of tractor diesel crawled across the room.

"Jaysus," Paddy said, wincing. "What's that?"

"You can smoke this, and that will a-fix you."

His hands hung over his head dramatically.

"Yeah, but what is it?"

"A psychedelic."

"Ah, psychedelics? I don't know if I'm in the mood. I've been on a three-day bender. I'll probably freak out." Lorenzo took out a syringe filled with liquid ketamine.

"No problemo," he said.

"Fuck me," Paddy replied. "You really think this is going to work?"

Lorenzo had no idea, but he was certain if he kept going the way he was going, his friend was going to kick the bucket on Christmas day.

"It's a drug?" Lorenzo was right. Paddy thought it was drugs. The most potent of all drugs, probably the great grandma of drugs, the mysterious psychedelic motherload, and he would have to smoke it. Now? Well, he was pretty close to suicide anyway.

What was another psychosis to add to the pile?

Paddy positioned himself on the couch, and Lorenzo loaded up a large bong shaped like a saxophone. He always thought it was funny when Lorenzo smoked the bong, which he did every five minutes, because it looked as if he was playing the sax. Paddy would laugh at Lorenzo, and Lorenzo would get paranoid about why he was laughing at him and kick him out.

Every damn time.

Lorenzo handed Paddy the pipe. Paddy felt butterflies in his stomach, as if he was about to go on the biggest rollercoaster in the world.

"Ready?" Lorenzo said and clicked the lighter like a starting pistol.

"Ok, ok. Hang on..." Paddy put his mouth on the pipe. *Here goes nothing,* he thought. Lorenzo lit the DMT, and Paddy inhaled the smoke cloud that he couldn't even really feel, like a long smoky tendril that faded into his soul. He fell backward, and suddenly, he was completely weightless, and the world fell apart, Tetris-style, into cubes. He entered the void.

He tried to scream, but no sound came out. His spirit travelled down a long tunnel at the speed of light, like a bullet, except he was aimed directly at a giant wall like a multicoloured mandala. He was certain he was going to crash into it!

"Nooooooo!" He tried to shout and then—*bang!*

The mandala shattered like a stained-glass window, and he came out the other side to raucous cheers and applause from some unseen, alien hands.

He was in some sort of suburban housing estate back in Ireland, not dissimilar to where he had grown up, except now, reality was a liquid. He had the feeling of being underwater, yet the scene was solid enough that in front of him, he could grab onto the long red banquet table.

What was this place? The table was solid enough to hold the silver dishes, candles, a roast dinner, and twenty people's plates, like an aristocratic Christmas dinner on acid.

The place felt familiar, as though he had been there before, maybe a million times, or perhaps forever. Maybe he had always been there. Paddy felt the edge of table cloth between his fingers, and thought about pulling it off to see what would happen.

"Stop," a calm but authoritative voice said. Paddy looked up, but didn't see anyone.

At the other end of the table was a mirror with his reflection in it, except his reflection was impeccably dressed in a tuxedo, hair combed neatly, skin clear and eyes precise and focused.

Paddy felt there was something evil about the reflection, the exact opposite of how he looked in reality, a doppelganger.

"Take a seat," the voice said from within the mirror.

Paddy noticed the mirror was wearing a suit, a black blazer, a white chemise, and a red cravat tie. The body had hands as wide as cinder blocks, wearing black leather gloves. It was clear that he was a man with a mirror for a face. Maybe, THE man with a mirror face.

"Who are you?" Paddy asked the mirror-faced man.

"I am you, and you are me. There are no differences, no questions, and only one answer..."

"Ah yes, that clears things up," Paddy said sarcastically and took a seat.

"We are about to eat." Paddy looked down at the plate covered in tiny pancakes, stacked like odd sea-stack rock formations.

"I'm not really hungry..." Paddy said. "What is this place?"

"The void... outer space... inner space... imagination... reality. Pick one, whatever one would make you more comfortable..."

"Well, why am I here then?"

"I thought you weren't hungry..."

"I mean, I didn't come for any specific reason. Lorenzo kind of made me. It's just my life is falling apart, and it's Christmas. I'm full of drugs, beer, and hopelessness. I just kind of yeno... Want to die." Paddy tasted one of the pancakes. It tasted like nothing.

"Don't eat those," the man with a mirror face said. "Who do you want to be, Paddy?"

"I don't know. Someone famous? Rich? An Emperor?"

For the first time, Paddy noticed the dancing elves that were everywhere. If he looked at the tablecloth for too long, they'd start oozing through the cracks in the particles and laughing and making fun of him. They multiplied and poured from every crevice of this reality. He didn't want a bad trip. He couldn't have one. A bad trip would literally kill him, he felt.

"You really shouldn't have eaten that pancake," the man with a mirror face said. Paddy didn't honestly know who he wanted to be.

He faced the mirror.

A great artist, he supposed. That could be it, something he could do.

"To be a great artist," Paddy said. "I want to create something really great!"

"Seems a little bit childish," the man with a mirror face said. 'Are you sure you wouldn't want a job? I could get you one in Tesco maybe, or Lidl? The benefits in Lidl are really quite good at the moment..."

"What?" Paddy scrunched up his face in the mirror. He wanted to be a great artist. That was the opposite of a job. That was the point of being an artist; you didn't have to work, and everybody loved you anyway. Work was the opposite of what he wanted!

"I don't want a job!" Paddy said, "I want to be an artist."

"Being an artist is a job," the man with a mirror face said,

"No, it's a pure expression of the soul! Free, unrestrained, uncontrollable!"

"Ah" the man with a mirror face said, "I see your problem, then, and I know what we need to do..."

"What then? I want to know!"

The man with a mirror face stood up from the table and wiped his crumbs from his suit. He was tall, probably over ten feet and intimidating, a towering giant.

"You need to let go of the past to move on with the future. I can show you. Only you can assemble the pieces and learn what you must to survive. I will show you three places: the past, the present, and the future..."

"Wait. Isn't that the plot of a Christmas Carol? Seems a little convoluted for this DMT trip. What am I, the Millennial Ebenezer Scrooge?"

"Look, this is your subconscious, Paddy, not mine..."

"Fine," Paddy said.

He walked around the table obediently and faced the mirror.

Paddy faced his perfect reflection, the same age, height, everything, like an evil twin brother who felt older and judgmental.

"What are you looking at?" Paddy said.

"I'm looking at myself," his reflection told him, and pulled him inside the man with a mirror face. Before Paddy knew what was happening, he was back in his childhood home in Ireland at Christmas, an expensive mansion in the south of Dublin with a long hallway and a marble staircase. It was a miracle! He recognised every inch of the old house which he had not been back to in years; the hall mirror, the green carpets, even the coat rack had the feeling of an old and long-forgotten friend. As a kid, he would hide in the coats during games of hide and go seek. He took hold of the oaken wooden frame and bent to smell the wood, a mixture of polish and mahogany, which brought back so many happy memories of excitement and competition.

What a treat! The Christmas decorations were already up, faux-holly and berries hanging from the ceiling. They entered the living room where a pile of presents was stacked up around the tree covered in red and golden baubles, with a pink angel on top.

All the presents were for him. Paddy was the only child of a wealthy family, the apple of his parents' eye, and Christmas was a time when he reaped the rewards.

"Why are we here?" Paddy asked. In the mirror, the reflection was younger, a girl, like a child with a glowing golden halo on her head. She looked eerie and unnatural, and he realised she was familiar, the girl who had died in the Tin Elephant. He had only met her once or twice in passing. Though the likeness changed, the more he looked, the more he could see his grandmother, aunties, uncles, anyone who had passed away.

"Who are you?"

"A doorway into the past, which is always changing, adapting."

"And why are we here?"

"For your salvation!"

"That sounds pretty heavy..."

A younger Paddy himself streaked through the scene, half-clothed with a screwdriver in his hand, banging and making noise like a jet airplane.

"Paddy, come back..." His mother called up the stairs. Paddy could nearly cry.

He was so real, this little child, so free, so perfect, so untroubled. What could have happened to him to make him such a rotten adult? This was where he would find the trauma that kept him trapped in his cycle of destruction, which destroyed his young spirit forever.

Who was to blame? His mother? His father? He vaguely remembered this day. What had happened since? In some sense, he knew this couldn't be real, that he was caught up in a hallucination, but his feeling was real. The excitement, the thrill—there was nothing fake about this emotion. Young Paddy pondered his presents, a touch of indecision on his brow, a twitch of uncertainty as his hand reached out and felt the red and green shining wrapping paper as if, like a blind man reading braille, he could divine what was underneath just by touch.

"Oh, for God's sake," Paddy said to his younger self, "just wait for the morning. Don't be such a pig!" Younger Paddy couldn't hear him.

"Feeling takes control of us and makes decisions of its own," the child with a mirror face said. Sure enough, young Paddy lost his battle with his desire and fell down greedily upon the largest of his presents.

"Of course," older Paddy said. His tearing of the paper unveiled a new Star Wars Lego set, one of the expensive ones from Smyths, which at the time in the late 90s would have cost more than fifty pounds, a Millennium Falcon. He was never any good at Lego anyway, lacking the patience to follow the directions and always ending up doing some half-aborted job of his own, for which he was highly praised.

"Paddy!" His mother came into the room to catch him, like a pig in the trough.

"Paddy, what are you doing?"

"They're my presents!" he said defensively, "I can open them whenever I want!" His mother was never much able to handle him whenever he put up a fight. He knew how to get around her, and since his father worked late, he could do mostly what he liked.

"Just listen to her," older Paddy said, exasperated with his younger self, "don't manipulate her. Just listen!"

"I want to open this one!"

"No Paddy, don't..." his mother cooed. "You have to wait until the morning."

"The morning is for Santa's presents. Why can't I open *your* ones tonight?"

She didn't have the strength to fight him, and most Christmases were like this. She was there alone, parent, Santa, guardian, and everything else.

"Ok fine, just one." Older Paddy shook his head as his younger self set about dismantling the present. He knew well what happened next. He would open another and another until the whole of Christmas was ruined, and then in the morning, he would moan and whine.

"Have you no spine!" He swore at his mother sitting next to him, watching her son with some forced glee, as if it was actually Christmas morning in her mind already.

"She loved you dearly, so she didn't want to see one moment of sadness on your face. That is better than most..." the child with a mirror face said wisely.

Older Paddy grumbled.

"She's the reason I'm like this."

"Do you think so?" the child with a mirror face said, leading him down the hallway.

Outside the landing window, Paddy watched the moon fall from the sky, like a shooting star. Then the sun rose and fell above half a dozen times, the two dancing, in the most miraculous display. His retinas were nearly scorched clear from his head, and his knees swayed with vertigo as if he were on the deck of a ship as time passed in an instant.

"Where are we now?" he asked the child with a mirror face, but the young girl was no longer there. In her place was a rotund man with long hair, bald on top, and a patchy brown beard. He had a giant belly and wore a bathrobe that let the fat mountain pop out.

"Welcome to the present, my dude!" He said it as if he was something like a John Belushi character and let out a great big hearty laugh.

"Go downstairs and get involved in the party."

Unlike the other girl, Paddy did not recognise this face in the mirror. He did not morph like she did, but only seemed to grow larger and larger the more you looked at him. Paddy walked down the stairs as he would have each Christmas morning when he was younger—when he still bothered to actually get up and wasn't crippled in bed with a hangover.

From inside the closed kitchen door, he could hear the sounds of mirth, plenty, and Frank Sinatra on the radio. He opened the doorway to see the whole family in action.

The kitchen table was set for a feast, and the whole family was there.

There were crackers, and hats, and jokes, aunties, uncles, grandparents, cousins; there must have been twenty in total. Paddy couldn't even remember having a Christmas like this when he was younger. In his mind, the memories had seemed so sparse, and yet here was something out of a medieval feast. His father and mother looked genuinely happy together as everyone gathered around the table with a ginormous turkey in the middle, and said a prayer.

"I almost wish I were there for this. It looks unbelievable. A far sight better than sitting in a stinking apartment in Germany with no family and only one friend."

His family finished their prayer and started eating.

"And what about young Paddy?" his grandmother trilled, "how is he?" Nobody ever told them anything. They were old and not to know all the trouble that went on behind closed doors but even then, my parents couldn't put up a front to lie to them. A shadow fell over their side of the dinner table at the mere mention of his name, and his father took a healthy draught of beer. From the way they were acting, you would swear he was dead or a murderer.

"I'm fine!" older Paddy said, "I mean, a little worse for wear but not that bad."

"We haven't heard from him in a while..." his mother said. "We have been worried. I mean, we are used to him disappearing, but this time, this last time, feels different."

His uncles and aunties shared a look. Suddenly, the food on the table looked less delicious, the spread sparser, as if the air was being let from the room, a deflating tyre.

"I'm sure he'll be fine, dear," his Dad said, "he's a smart kid. He'll find his own way back." This seemed to be good enough for everyone, and older Paddy felt tears come to his eyes. His dad had always believed in him, no matter what.

"I'm not so sure, Dad..." Paddy said, feeling the sadness and melancholy which clung to his bones, engulfing the room like a sandstorm, "I feel pretty much done for..."

The mirthful man in the mirror stretched, and expanded, and yawned.

"The party will do that to you, my dude, you sink deeper and deeper into a dream which becomes a reality, and you can't live without the heat like me..." Suddenly, Paddy realised who he was, the mirthful man. He was the large fat man who had hung himself in the Tin Elephant, where he had been found on the bannisters, resting like a bloated Christmas decoration. A testament to sadness and German engineering. Lorenzo had known him and said he was the life and soul of every party. No-one ever suspected that anything so dark could be going on underneath. From within the mirror, the mirthful man lifted a squealing pig under one arm and a half-frazzled cat, which looked like it had been electrocuted, under the other.

"These are your pets," he said, "greed and fear. You let them run the show, and you won't get very far. You are a father of sorts yourself already." Paddy had never thought of it like that. His own father seemed a forceful but distant character. He watched him there at the table, smiling, playing, laughing. He never felt as if he wanted to emulate him before now.

"And what are you doing with yourself, young Timmy, in this economy?" his father said, and his cousin raised his head from his phone. His young cousin flushed red with the table's attention on him, something Paddy was not particularly fond of himself. His cousin had grown up so much to be a fine young man on the point of leaving school and beginning his life.

"Just finishing school really..." He did not elaborate.

There were a great many things Paddy wanted to tell him, advice and caution about the future. But then again, who was he? Who was he going to be? The words of the man with a mirror face came back to him: who do you want to be?

"Merry Christmas, everyone!" His cousin said in a rare moment of confidence, and everyone raised a glass in salute.

"I'd like to stay, but the final destination awaits, my dude," the mirthful man with a mirror face said, beckoning Paddy to come with him.

They left the kitchen, descending into the basement of the house.

In his younger days, Paddy had been scared of the basement; it was dark and concrete, but now the room was different. It looked just like Paddy's apartment in the Tin Elephant, piled high with filth, dirty clothes, beer bottles, and half-eaten pizza, stinking and rotting, a stark contrast from the warmth and company of the present which he had just experienced.

He was almost annoyed to be back in his old haunt and longed for the order, for the cleanliness. There he was on the bed, chubby with a stupid expression on his face. He looked much older, maybe four or five years, fat and unhappy.

"Twenty-seven," a person in the mirror gurgled. Paddy recognised him. He was the DJ who had choked to death on his own vomit. The truth was he was actually friends with Paddy. They were both artists, in a way, men who loved creation, freedom, and chaos. The DJ's neck was wide and bloated, filled with the bile and vomit which killed him, so he could barely speak. Paddy didn't know why he did not just clear it. Why did he let it sit there?

"Twenty-seven," he said again, the age at which the DJ had died, and also so many rock stars: Jim Morrison, Jimmy Hendrix, Kurt Cobain. There was something romantic about the youthful destruction, the early poetic death, self-immolation before you lived long enough to become the villain, *the man.* Paddy could see his youthful exuberance had faded.

The last of his golden youth was dried up and gone.

He was instead left with a decaying corpse of a body that he had run into the ground. The flies hovered over him and dive-bombed his skin, but he took no notice of them, sleeping in on this Christmas morning. There was a knocking on the door, probably Lorenzo, coming to wake him up. Except instead of his friend, when the door opened, two police came in.

"Twenty-seven," the DJ said again. His eyes were cold and unstaring, impersonal. There was not one drop of humanity left in him, no mercy, no second chance—death personified.

The police walked over and checked his pulse on his mattress without sheets.

One shook his head. The other looked around the room, disgusted.

Paddy remembered when his friend, the DJ, had died, the police had come and drawn a chalk outline around him, and that brown stain was all that had been left in the end.

His parents would be called, given the news: dead, abroad, at twenty-seven.

"Twenty-seven," the DJ echoed. Paddy collapsed to his knees, holding his dead body.

"I just want to live! I want to live!" he said out of desperation, "is that too much to ask for?"

He looked up to see the man with a mirror face had returned, his older, more judgmental reflection. The man with a mirror face looked down on him,

"You must leave the boy behind. Lest that stinking corpse becomes your fate."

"I'm sorry... I'm sorry... I'll do anything, please..."

He felt his strength leaving him, as if a dream were dying away. He, Paddy, was dying with it. His words, his apologies were too late. His throat was closing, and he couldn't breathe.

He was choking. He would wander like the shades within the mirror forever, warning others who were to head down the same road as him. He could see the girl, the mirthful man, the DJ above him. He closed his eyes and expected to drift away forever. Except instead, like holy Italian Jesus above him with a bald tennis ball head, he saw Lorenzo.

"Estupido Paddy!" Lorenzo swore. "Let go! Let go!"

Paddy let go of the dead boy he was holding and fell back; he felt a pop. Suddenly, air flooded in from every corner of the Earth. Choking, sputtering, he returned to the room which he had left only a moment before.

"Lorenzo! Lorenzo!" he shouted, kissing his friend on the cheek, "it's a fucking Christmas miracle. You saved my life!"

"Too a-fucking right," Lorenzo said. "You are a-choking on your tongue? You turn white, then a-purple, then a-green-a. I thought you were a-dying?" Paddy shook his head, feeling clearer about things than he ever had; freer.

"I think I did..." Paddy jumped up and had a scour around the room for his shoes, stuffing his feet into the crusted Nikes.

"What are you doing?" Lorenzo asked him,

"It's Christmas," Paddy said, "I have to call my parents. We need a turkey. We can't let this night go to waste Lorenzo!" Paddy felt as if he had a job, a purpose, a story to tell.

Lorenzo smiled up at his friend.

"Paddy, maybe you-a no so *estupido*, after all.."

About the Author

Photograph @grahamcrichton.

Mahon McCann is an Irish author, blogger, playwright and martial artist.

Born and raised in Dublin, Ireland, he graduated from University College, Dublin with a BA in Economics and Philosophy (2016) and then went on to obtain his MA in Creative Writing from Queens University in Belfast (2019), where he now resides.

He fights professionally in Muay Thai and has been involved in western boxing and Bujinkan Ninjutsu from an early age. In his spare time, he volunteers with Fighting Words Belfast at a weekly write club for creative teens.

His interests include philosophy, psychology, religion, stories, relationships and masculinity. For his blog and upcoming projects, see his website and mailing list at: www.mahonmccann.com, his Instagram @mahon_mccann and his Facebook author's page @mahonmccann.

Thanks for reading!
Please add a review on Amazon and let me
Know what you think!

Amazon reviews are extremely helpful for authors,
thank you for taking the time to support me and
my work. Don't forget to share your review on social media
with the hashtag #themanwithamirrorface and
encourage others to read the stories too!

Printed in Great Britain
by Amazon